ENCHANTING HER MATE

ALIENS OF OLUURA

BOOK SIX

IVY KNOX

AUTHOR'S NOTE

If you don't have any concerns regarding content and how it may affect you, **feel free to skip ahead to avoid spoilers!**

This book contains scenes that either reference or include verbal abuse, graphic violence, as well as substance abuse, which may be triggering for some. If you or someone you know is in need of support, there are places you can go for help. I have listed some resources at the end of this book.

****This is a story about a same-sex couple falling in love. If that's not for you, please stop reading now.**

CHAPTER 1

JOBAKI "JO"

Untamed, reckless sorceress. That is what I have become. The shame of my reputation weighs on me like a thick cloak, surrounding me at all times.

"A liability to the clan." "A Hexrin who cannot be trusted." These are the thoughts that swept through the minds of my coven when I left the clan and retreated to Kayt and Nee-roh's home in the caves.

I do not blame the coven for thinking such things. It is my fault dear Nalba, our brilliant inventor, was badly injured in the battle against Bzzsil Chi and his henchmen. I tried to save our clan by using my fire orb against Bzzsil, and if Tibik had not interfered, I am quite sure I would have been successful. Bzzsil Chi would have died by my hand, and Nalba would never have been hit by mistake and thrown into that tree, causing her to lose her memories.

I have not spoken to Tibik since the battle. After Nalba was taken to the healer for her head injury, he took the opportunity to scream at me in front of the other members of the coven, "If Nalba dies, it is on your hands. You are not strong enough to attempt such advanced spells. Shame on you for thinking otherwise." I did not offer a response. I just left. And his words have followed me to the caves.

It has been many days since Nee-roh and Kayt brought me here, but the pain feels fresh, even though leaving was the right choice. I must take this time away from the clan to hone my powers and control them fully before I return.

"Hey, Jo. You busy?" Kayt asks as she leans against the door of my room.

"I am not," I tell her. Silently punishing myself for Nalba's injury can wait until later.

Kayt does a gleeful hop in place at my words. "Oh good! Come, come." She gestures for me to follow her down the hall to the room with the giant machine that helps her make clothes. I believe she calls it a digital stitcher. When we arrive, she pulls a garment from a hook near the door and holds it in front of me.

She tilts her head from side to side as she examines it. "Hmm, it might be a little loose on you, but I think the color will look fantastic with your skin and that maroon hair. Try it on for me?"

"Yes, I shall," I reply, taking the garment behind the black velvet curtain Kayt has hung in the corner of the room and removing my tunic and leggings. Many members of my clan are quite comfortable with nudity, but that is not a sentiment I share. Due to my unusually small size, I am not often pleased with the look of my body. Kayt even assumed that I was a young girl when we first met.

The dress Kayt fashioned for me is quite nice once I have it on, but there are two long pieces of the smooth teal fabric that hang off my back and chest, and I am not sure what to do with them. "Is this correct?" I ask, upon stepping out from behind the curtain.

"Let me fix that," Kayt says, lightly slapping away my hands. She takes the two pieces and ties them into a fluffy bow that sits atop my shoulder. Then she tugs at the bottom hem of the dress until it reaches my knees, and the bunched fabric at my stomach is smoothed out.

When she takes a step back to look at me, her hands fly to her face, covering her mouth. "Oh my god, Jo, you look amazing!"

Kayt nudges me to the large mirror propped against the wall, and the moment I look into it, my breath becomes lodged in my throat. I have never worn anything like this. In my five centuries, I have never worn a garment that reveals so much skin. My arms are bare, there is a cut-out showing the area of skin just beneath my breasts, and the bodice and skirt are quite tight. They are not too tight for the dress to fit, or for me to breathe, but the dress is tighter than my usual loose tunic and leggings. Those tend to hang off my small frame. This… does not.

"I do not know about this," I tell her honestly. I do not wish to hurt Kayt's feelings. She has made a gorgeous garment, but it does not feel quite like me.

"Oh, come on," Kayt protests. "You look absolutely stunning. Besides, you should take more fashion risks." Then her green eyes light up in a way that makes it clear I am not winning this battle. "I would have so much fun building you a wardrobe."

Before I can offer a counterpoint, Nee-roh pokes his head into the room. "Ah, hello, my *rivi*," he says to Kayt. Then his eyes meet mine in the mirror. "I see my mate has recruited you for a bit of dress-up. How nice. Hopefully this will deter her from removing any more items from my closet."

"Everything you own is black," Kayt replies with a groan. "Don't get me wrong, black is my favorite color too, but let me bring some patterns into your life, blue man."

Nee-roh shrugs. "I am famished," he says. "Would you two care to join me for a meal?"

"Oh, you know I'm always down to eat," Kayt says. "Especially with my little fire-breather here." She rubs a hand over the lower part of her belly that is just starting to show signs of her pregnancy.

"That would be lovely," I reply, sighing as I watch Kayt toss my tunic and leggings into the bucket of cleansing solution. It seems I have no choice but to keep this very revealing dress on.

Kayt and Nee-roh set our usual places at the long table in the center of the eating room, with them sitting beside each other on one side, and me on the other. Our meal is a bowl of steaming *rofan mash* with chunks of *kuhnypa meat* on top smothered in a spicy brown sauce. I have grown to adore this dish.

"Thank you for this," I tell them.

Kayt immediately groans. "You don't have to thank us for every single meal, Jo. You're our guest, but we want you to feel comfortable here. Like this is your home too."

"Though, perhaps more like a second home, rather than a primary place of residence," Nee-roh clarifies as he takes a bite. He is a polite and kind male, for the most part, but it is quite clear that he would prefer to have the caves, and his mate, to himself.

"Of course," I reply with a smile. I am grateful they have allowed me to stay. If not for their hospitality, I would be forced to endure Tibik's wrath over what happened. His loud, angry rants would echo through the house we share with the rest of the coven, making them uncomfortable. Space is best for us right now.

The door to the launch room slams shut, and the three of us turn our heads toward the sound. "Brother! I am here!" Nee-roh rolls his eyes upon hearing the greeting, and moments later, Alu appears in the doorway of the eating room.

"Ah, I am so relieved I did not miss mealtime," she says with a smile as she saunters to the food dispenser and presses buttons on the control panel.

Nee-roh clears his throat. "Sister, what a surprise. I do not recall inviting you to join us for mealtime."

"You did not," she says without turning around. "But I know I am always welcome here in your caves."

Nee-roh stares at his sister's back, his mouth twisted into a deep scowl. "Is that so?"

Kayt lightly smacks Nee-roh's forearm. "Of course you are, Alu." She turns to Nee-roh and holds his gaze while adding, "*We* love having you here."

Nee-roh rubs a hand down his face, looking positively exhausted. "Yes, it is a joy to see you."

Alu takes her steaming bowl of rofan mash and settles into the seat to my right. It is then that she takes in my attire, and her eyes widen as they travel along my body. "Jobaki," she says, slightly breathless, "you look…exquisite."

My stomach flutters at her words as heat fills my chest. It is a reaction I was not expecting, though I am also not entirely surprised by.

"Doesn't she look like a total smoke show?" Kayt asks, shooting me a wink. "I made that dress."

"Brilliant work, dear sister," Alu says, never taking her gaze off me.

Instinctually, I place a hand over the exposed skin beneath my breasts as blood rushes to my cheeks. "I-I thank you, Alu. That is kind of you to say."

We settle into a companionable quiet as we eat our meals, though I find it difficult to focus on the food. It is a delicious dish, but I find the room has grown hot since Alu arrived, and I am continuously distracted by the way her lips move as she chews. How can the act of chewing be so very sensual?

I remember sharing a heated moment with Alu at Kayt's day of birth celebration not too long ago. It was a dark, chilly eve, and she found me standing alone at the edge of where all the dancing was taking place. She strolled right up to me and demanded I follow her to a nearby bench. My body listened even before my mind could protest, and we sat together under the soft light of the douku orbs in the trees above, talking about everything and nothing at all.

When she leaned in, presumably to kiss me, it felt as if my heart was about to burst through my chest. Then Nee-roh got into an argument with Bruvix, and the moment was lost.

There was another time, more recently, at a previous dinner in these very caves, that she held my hand beneath the table and stroked her thumb across my palm. Even that sent a chill down my spine.

"Are you enjoying your stay with my brother and his mate, Jo?" Alu asks, jolting me out of my memories.

"Uh, it has been a nice time, yes," I mutter, nervously moving my utensil in a circle through the mash. "I am taking this opportunity to focus on my craft."

"How delightful," Alu exclaims.

She is unlike anyone I have met in my five centuries. Alu has a unique openness and curiosity about the world around her. I find it quite refreshing. It is a stark contrast to Tibik's suffocating pessimism which often created a sour atmosphere among the coven.

"I could certainly use your powers at my home in the jungle," she says with a huff. "Mek, my feathered friend, is not well."

"Oh no. Mek's sick?" Kayt asks, creases forming on her brow.

Alu tilts her head to the side. "Not sick, exactly."

"Who is Mek?" I ask, my voice taking on a harsher tone than expected. Jealousy unfurls in the depths of my gut as I wonder how Alu knows this Mek. I have not felt this emotion in many moons. It is unsettling to be feeling it now.

Nee-roh takes a sip of *tibbi* and then sets his glass on the table with a heavy sigh. "Mek is a filthy bird my sister foolishly allows into her home." He turns to Alu. "You would not have to worry about that creature being sick if you forced it to live outside in the jungle where it belongs."

"I am not foolish!" she shouts, slamming the end of her utensil against the table. She quickly composes herself, though her chest still heaves. "Mek is my friend. I will not turn him away."

Alu places her hand on top of mine, and I freeze. Her skin is so soft, and the warmth of her palm spreads throughout my entire body. "Please, Jobaki. I believe Mek is possessed by an ancient spirit. Only you can save him."

"An ancient spirit? Truly?" Nee-roh scoffs.

Alu nods solemnly.

"It is possible," I tell him. "We are surrounded by the energies of those who have come before us. Perhaps Mek's mind is a portal for those who wish to communicate from beyond their resting place, much like Kayt's mind is."

"But what kind of dumbass ghost would send their message through a bird?" Kayt asks, chuckling.

"I do not know, sister," Alu replies, mystified. She seems to be completely unaware of the hint of mockery in Kayt's voice.

"I can certainly try connecting my mind to his to see what ails him," I tell Alu. "Though I am not sure I will be of much help beyond that."

Alu drops her utensil with a loud clatter as she claps her hands excitedly. "Wonderful! We shall depart after we eat."

"Oh, you wish to go this eve?" I ask, suddenly aware of the fact that Alu's house is not close by, so she will have to shift into her draxilio to fly us there, and the only clean clothing I have is the revealing dress I am currently wearing.

"Yes, I do not feel right about leaving him alone while he is suffering," she says.

That is understandable.

Though it means I will be in her home, alone. Aside from Mek, it will be the two of us, and with the way Alu's heated gaze continues to linger on my bare arms and chest, I am worried I will not be able to keep myself away from her. I have been celibate for over two centuries, and Alu is a temptation I did not see coming.

"Very well," I reply.

"Good," Alu says, triumph in her tone as she tosses her long, silky black mane over her shoulder. "You shall stay with me until we can determine what is happening with poor Mek."

"Certainly." What have I just agreed to?

CHAPTER 2

ALUSSANAI "ALU"

By the time we arrive at my home, it is the middle of the night. *Makka nei,* I wish my brother, Nirossanai, or Niro, as Kate calls him, lived closer. I do not mind flying in the dark; it is just that I am eager to have Jo in my home so I may finally taste her lips.

I have longed to press my mouth to hers since the moment we met at Kate's day of birth celebration, and I still have not had the opportunity to do so. At this point, I want her so badly, I can barely breathe.

Perhaps I should feel remorse for bringing her here under false pretenses, but how else was I supposed to spend time alone with her? Back in the clan of golden ones, Jo lives in a crowded home with several others—her "coven," as she calls it. While staying in Niro's caves is certainly better in terms of fewer people hovering around her, I am not comfortable seducing her there with my brother and his mate nearby.

Kate has told me that Jo struggles with the events that unfolded during the battle against Bzzsil Chi, but I have yet to discuss this with Jo, and I am eager to remind her that Nalba's injury is not her fault, but with Kate and Niro always hovering, I have not had the chance.

I had to lie about Mek being possessed by an ancient spirit so she would leave my brother's caves altogether and come to my home. I do not know how long it will take Jobaki to figure out Mek is not ailing. He is just a strange, ornery bird of the jungle who makes his nest in the pillows of my spare bed. She will probably discover my ruse immediately, as she is quite smart. Much smarter than I am.

I hope she will not be too angry with me.

Truthfully, I have grown tired of people—my brothers—always being angry with me. It seems there is not a task I can complete without doing something wrong. They often tell me how gullible or simpleminded I am because of my genetic modifications. But it is not as if I chose to exist without the ability to feel fear. Our handlers chose this life for me by altering my brain tissue. If I could reverse the calcification on the part of my brain that registers fear, I would in an instant.

What does fear feel like? It is a question I have pondered many times. I imagine it would be thrilling to have your mind warning you not to do something before you do it. There are no warning signals in my head before I do anything, so I am often scolded for actions my brothers deem "too dangerous" or "foolish."

While my brothers also suffer with their own genetic modifications—Niro lacks remorse, Bexo lacks trust, and Kuli lacks awe—they do not mock each other the same way they mock me.

If I can show them my lack of fear does not mean I am lacking in intelligence, perhaps their mockery will cease. And is luring the most beautiful sorceress on Oluura to my home to free my bird from the clutches of an ancient spirit not a brilliant plan? It took many days for me to hatch this scheme of mine, and I am quite proud of the results thus far.

They shall regret their foolish words! my draxilio shouts triumphantly inside my head. The bond with my draxilio is sacred, as we both occupy this body. I let her out when I shift into my other form, the one that can fly and breathe fire, and while I am in my flightless form, she is encouraging me to behave as she would, to be bolder and more confident. Most things excite her, so her voice is often a shout inside my head.

Should Jo decide she is not interested in me, I shall return her to Niro's caves at once without hesitation or complaint. But I do not think that will happen. I feel her eyes following me whenever I am near, and the addicting floral scent of her arousal blooms in the air the moment my skin touches hers. She wants this as desperately as I do.

I shift into my flightless form the moment we land outside the tunnel that leads to my cottage, and I find Jo shivering to the point where I worry she may faint. "Are you well?" I ask, coming to stand in front of her.

Her fangs clatter loudly as she shivers. "I-It is just q-quite cold, and th-th-this dress does nothing to protect m-my skin."

Goodness, I had not even considered how the wind would whip through my claws as I flew with Jo tucked inside. This poor female. I have not properly cared for her at all.

The cold season is most severe where Niro's caves are located, and though the air does hold a chill here in the jungle as well, it is not as brutal. Her body should adjust to the warmer temperature soon enough, but how will I get her through the tunnel if she can barely stand?

Not knowing what else to do, I wrap my arms around her and pull her flush against my body. She is a small creature, her head barely reaching the middle of my chest. I am hoping my larger size will provide enough warmth to keep her alive until we arrive at my home.

"Shh," I whisper in an attempt to comfort her, as I rub my hands up and down her arms. Then I recall a phrase I read in a book when I was a child. It was something natural-born draxilio mothers would say to their young when they were afraid.

"Vana kiyle tu benof charchery vunup xi hulliya bo wqikiva. Kukuvai qpi mussaw kwe dinl sah ul nuzilba."

"When the shadow of the unknown chills you to the bone, stand strong. The fire in your heart will forever keep you warm."

I feel the goose bumps fade from Jo's bare skin at my words. Her body loosens as I hold her, and her hands end up splayed on my lower back. I briefly wonder how she could possibly still be cold when my skin feels like it is on fire.

She pulls back enough to look me in the eye. "That was beautiful. What is it from?"

I am confused. "You understand Sufoian?"

"Of course," she says plainly.

"It is, uh," I stammer, still shocked she knows the language of my home planet. "It is from a book." My mind wanders as I envision a female draxilio leaning down to the height of her child and uttering those words in a soft voice. "The phrase always made me happy. I sometimes wished I could feel fear, just to have it said to me."

Jo's big gold eyes swirl with…something I do not recognize.

"You deserved to hear such comforting words," she finally says. "I am sorry you did not."

Pity. It was pity.

That is not what I want my soon-to-be lover's eyes to hold. This scheme is going terribly thus far.

"Yes, well," I say, releasing her from my grasp. "We should go check on Mek, yes?" I gesture for her to follow me as we enter the tunnel. "Apologies that it is so very dark in here. I must add a light of some kind."

Despite my apology, I see fairly well in the dark. Though, when a long, black *vinepus* slithers across the toe of Jobaki's boot and she screams, it becomes abundantly clear to me that she cannot see as well as I.

"Do not worry," I tell her, placing a hand on her forearm. "It is merely a vinepus. They are not friendly, but they are also not vicious."

"I suppose that is good," she whispers, grabbing my hand and lacing her fingers through mine.

My skin tingles at the contact as a smile tugs at the corners of my lips. We walk the rest of the way through the tunnel like this, and I struggle to resist the urge to back her against the stone wall of the tunnel and kiss all over her neck and chest. I have spent far too many nights wondering what her skin tastes like, what her nipples look like, and what kind of sounds she would make as I pleasure her.

She will not be able to resist you! my draxilio adds. *You are magnificent!*

But I cannot lose control now. Not before we make it to my cottage. I want my first kiss with Jobaki to be in the light, so she can see how deeply I desire her.

"Ah, at last," she says with a relieved sigh as we step onto the narrow dirt path that shall take us the rest of the way.

I guide her around to the front of my cottage and smile the moment the lime green pebbles that fill my walkway come into view. "We are home," I tell her as I slide the heavy brown front door to the side.

"My," she says, letting go of my hand as hers flies to her mouth. "Oh, my." She looks around my home in wonder. "It is so spacious and lovely."

Mek's prickly chirp sounds from down the hall. He has been asleep in the spare bedroom, I am sure, and is not pleased with the late-night interruption to his slumber.

"Oh, hello," Jo says sweetly as Mek darts around the main room, his red-feathered wings slicing through the air as he dips and turns. When his three eyes land on Jo, he pivots quickly and flies toward her, crashing right into the side of her head. She falls to the ground, eyes closed.

My draxilio gasps at the same time I do. *That is not good! Mek has ruined the mood!*

"Mek!" I shout as he shakes his tiny bird head and flies back down the hall.

I crouch over Jo's unconscious body, leaning next to her lips to ensure she is still breathing. She is, and her heartbeat remains strong, which is a massive relief, but this is not the smooth courtship I envisioned. Not at all.

CHAPTER 3

JO

$\mathcal{I}$ wake to the feel of something cold and wet on my forehead and the soft murmurs of Alu's voice promising me all will be well. My eyelids flutter open, and I find myself on a deep, circular couch the color of hot embers.

"Ah, you awaken," Alu says, her smile wide despite the tightness of her features. "Good. This is very good."

She gives me space to sit up, and as soon as I do, the room spins.

"Move slowly," Alu cautions me.

"What happened?"

The look on Alu's face tells me it is something she does not wish to relive. Eventually, she sighs and her shoulders slump down. "Mek flew into your head. I am sorry for his terribly rude behavior." She snarls when she turns to face the bird, who is perched behind her on the back of the couch, looking positively unbothered.

His three eyes blink at me and his head tilts back and forth as if he is trying to figure out if I am a friend or foe. He is quite pretty to look at. The deep red feathers that cover his body have a slight shimmer, making it appear as if thin blue streaks are within them.

"I am not here to cause you harm, sweet fellow," I tell him. "I came to help you."

Alu continues addressing Mek directly. "She came all this way from the clan of the golden ones, Mek! Stop embarrassing me."

Mek squawks back with a loud, piercing pitch as if arguing with Alu. Though I suppose that is the ancient spirit trying to communicate. Poor little creature. It must be so frightening to have another presence invading one's mind. I must help him, but I am not certain I have the strength or the focus to solve this problem this late in the eve.

"Would it be possible to exorcise the spirit inside Mek tomorrow?" I ask Alu. "I am quite tired from the journey."

"Certainly," Alu replies. "Come along, little menace," she says as she pats her shoulder. Mek hops from the couch to Alu's shoulder, his claws digging into her glowing cerulean skin. He is quite large, almost too large to fit on Alu's shoulder, but it seems as if he is unaware of his massive size. She disappears down the hall, presumably to the spare room he occupies.

She returns soon after, and I feel my heart skip at the sight of her entering the room. Her long black mane is swept up into a ponytail, showing off the intricate dark blue tattoo etched into the shaved side of her head. Her hips sway enticingly with each step, and though she is covered in lean muscle, her thighs jiggle and her breasts bounce with each movement. The black horns that jut out of her head are wide at the base and dangerously sharp at the ends, making her look like the most lethal predator one could encounter in the jungle. Perhaps she is.

Her soft smile gives her away, however. There is no one on Oluura, or anywhere else, for that matter, with a warmer heart than Alu. She is so much more than she seems.

"Your home is quite lovely," I tell her, clearing my throat and trying to push away the thoughts of her that will surely cause my knees to buckle the moment I stand.

"I thank you," she says with a nod. "I believe that is what you were about to say before my bird collided with your face."

We both chuckle as she helps me to my feet.

"I have another spare room across from mine that you may use," she says as I follow her down the hall.

"I thought I would be sharing with Mek."

She laughs, the sound uninhibited and loud. Not the least bit dignified. It is a sound I immediately become addicted to. "I would pull you into my bed long before I would allow that to happen."

The moment the words leave her mouth, a loaded silence builds between us like a wall; requiring a bold action from one or both of us to tear it down.

"Well, I must rest," I tell her after waiting what feels like an eternity to see if she would kiss me.

"Are you certain you should sleep with a head wound?" she asks, pointing to the large bump just beneath my hairline.

"Ah, it is no bother," I tell her. I wave my hand over the area as my eyelids close. Then I concentrate on the color of the injury—a bright, concerning shade of pink—to dull the color. I feel the pain slowly evaporate as the tint softens, and eventually, disappears altogether.

Alu's gray eyes widen as she leans in close to examine my head wound. "Did you just heal yourself?"

"I did, yes," I tell her with a nod. "It is a limited power, however. I can only heal myself, not others, and if the wound is severe, I will not have enough energy to mend it."

"Fiyana!" she shouts. My translator chip indicates the meaning of this Sufoian phrase is "incredible." She opens the door to the spare room and gestures for me to enter. "I am astounded by your power, Jo."

I smile at the compliment but hastily add, "That is kind of you, but my power is an uncontrollable burden at the moment. It is not the impressive attribute you think it to be."

Before I can take a step into the room, Alu grabs my arm. "No, Jobaki. Your power is what makes you a spectacular creature. You do not need to be in tune with it for it to be an impressive part of you. It is only one of many extraordinary parts of you."

A shiver shoots across my skin as Alu's gaze holds mine. I do not know what to say. Though I am quite certain I have never been on the receiving end of such kind words in the five centuries my soul has been inside this body. "I…" I stammer then clear my throat, "I thank you, Alu."

She smiles, showing off her white, pointy teeth. They are not the sharp fangs I have, but between the blunt squares humans have and the fangs all Trovilians possess.

"I am glad you were able to stay with Kate and Niro before coming here," she says, leaning against the door. Then she lets out a dreamy sigh. "Seeing my brother happily mated is such a gift. I hope the rest of us podlings are able to find our mates one day. Our 'inaras.' That is the term you use in the village for mates, yes?"

"Historically, the term 'inara' is reserved for the female mates of male Trovilians," I explain. "It refers to the story of our creation when Goddess Ruhveena saved our people in a battle to the death with the Gods Buhno, Mikaroh, and Danik. The gods were in an endless struggle for power that lasted centuries, and when she defeated Buhno and Mikaroh, Danik was so grateful to be spared that he devoted himself to her entirely. She became his reason for living, a reminder of all that is good and right in the galaxy."

Alu tilts her head as if lost in thought. Then her voice lowers as she asks, "Does this mean it is not common among your people to see romantic partners of the same sex?"

"No, no," I reply. "There are many pairings on Trovilia who did not fit this classic template of eternal mates. It is not as if our people were forbidden from taking a mate of the same sex or remaining with them until the final rest. But the title of 'inara' simply was not used outside male-female mated pairs."

"Ah," Alu replies, nodding. "Well, enjoy your slumber." Then she turns, striding down the hall toward her room, the soft globes of her behind jiggling as she goes, leaving me breathless.

When I climb beneath the thick, warm blankets and blissfully sink into the deep cushions of Alu's spare bed, I cannot shake the tingling that lingers on my skin where Alu grabbed my arm and offered the kindest words I have ever heard. It keeps me awake much longer than I would prefer despite the feeling of electric desire that continues to shoot through me. Could she be…my inara?

No, no, that is not possible.

Hexrins are forbidden from taking a mate while serving their coven, Tibik reminds us more often than is necessary. It is as if stating the policy fills him with glee. He tells us that we are mated to our magic, and if taking a mate becomes a higher priority than our coven, we will be expelled immediately.

This has always seemed like an antiquated and ridiculous policy to enforce as Hexrins have the capacity to remain engaged and loyal to their covens while taking a mate. Cruvo, a Hexrin who remained on Trovilia when we left and is mated to Queen Ekoya, was the first to disobey this policy. He was shunned for a long time after completing the mating ceremony with Ekoya, but as he is now the queen's mate, every coven on Trovilia wants him to join and have even offered him the role of Prime, which is leader of a coven.

My coven does not know I am the Prime Hexrin. Tibik and I agreed when we settled on Oluura that he would assume the role of Prime, despite my power being much stronger than his. Tibik comes alive when all eyes are on him, whereas I shrink. It is what made me think he would be the best leader for our coven. It seemed like a smart arrangement at the time, but over the years, he seems to have forgotten that it is merely a ruse.

If, and when, I am able to control my power, I will return to the coven. Facing Tibik will be inevitable, and we will need to decide how to proceed after the mishap during the battle. If I claim my role as Prime, perhaps my first decree should be that Hexrins are free to take a mate.

* * *

The sound of screams and water splashing fill the room, and I am yanked out of a peaceful slumber. With blurred vision and stiff limbs, I tumble out of bed and race to the window. My room overlooks the rocky cliffs beneath Alu's home and the waterfall that feeds into a pool of crystal-clear water below. Alu's blue face pops out of the water, her horns and hair splashing behind her as she swims around the pool.

I let out a breath I did not realize was stuck in my throat.

She spots me in the window and waves, her white fangs a stark contrast to the color of the water. Then I see her head dip below the surface briefly before her draxilio bursts into the air. Water streams from every corner of her wide blue wings as she flaps them and flies to the top of the cliffs.

Mek squawks in a much happier tone as he flies above my head, leading me down the hall toward the main room of Alu's home. Alu meets us there in her flightless form. She stands in the middle of the wood floor between the main room and the eating room, completely naked, as a puddle of water forms around her feet.

"How was your slumber?" she asks brightly as she wraps her mane around her wrist and squeezes out the excess water, not caring about the amount of liquid that forms on the floor.

Not only am I mesmerized by her bare skin, but the way in which Alu occupies each space she enters. Her mind works in unique ways. Where something like water spilling onto the floor would be a concern for many, it is not for her. I am envious of that mental freedom.

My eyes travel down her long, elegant neck, landing on her chest. The sight of her breasts on display has me licking my lips. They are smaller than the human females, but larger than my own, making me picture how they would look filling my palms. Her nipples are pebbled and in a darker shade of blue than her skin. I wonder what it would feel like to close my lips around them and slowly trace each one with the tip of my tongue.

"Jo?" Alu says, tilting her head to the side as she stares at me.

Oh goddess, I have been caught.

She clears her throat and nods knowingly, then steps into the eating room to grab something before returning. Alu throws a garment over her head, and it loosely falls around her lean, muscular frame. It is a lightweight, shapeless dress in an olive-green shade with a small knot tied at the hem, hitting just above her right knee. "Apologies. I am usually nude at home, as it is just me here."

"Ah, it is…fine," I mumble, unsure of what to say. Perhaps it would have been better to say nothing at all. It is not as if I can act on even the smallest flicker of desire. If I cannot take a mate, what is the point?

"Mek!" Alu shouts with a wide smile as the bird flies toward her, landing on her shoulder.

"I should, uh, I-I can connect with his energy now," I offer, trying to push away the image of her nipples in my mind. "If this is a good time, that is."

The confidence that always seems present in her gray eyes wavers, but only for a moment. "Yes," she replies, her tone slightly nervous. "Yes, now is a splendid time."

We sit next to each other on the overstuffed orange couch in the sunken part of the main room, and I hold out a finger for Mek. He stares at my hand as if it is a snack, but then he leaps from Alu's shoulder to my finger, his thick claws wrapping all the way around it.

"All right," I say as I close my eyes and open myself to his energy. I take three deep breaths as I focus on the weight of his body on my hand, and I start to feel the rapid but strong, beat of his heart through his claws. Soon I am able to see the state of his organs, the blood pumping to his heart, and the shape of his small bones.

Under my breath, I recite the spell that allows me to enter the mind of another, and the moment I finish, I am able to see what Mek sees through each of his three eyes. When I enter his mind, I do not find the signature cloudiness of a spirit who is desperate to communicate a message. I find nothing but thoughts about berries and nests.

Silently, I release his mind and close the link to his energy. He lifts off my hand, and I hear his wings flapping as he flies away. When I open my eyes, Alu looks quite strange. Her gaze is unfocused as she stares at something off in the distance. I wonder what caused her to think her bird was possessed. Mek seems to behave like a wild creature of the jungle, but that should not surprise her.

"Alu," I begin, trying to figure out the best way to proceed. "I do not thi–"

My words are cut off as Alu presses her lips to mine.

CHAPTER 4

ALU

Jo tastes better than her scent, which I was not expecting because her scent is magnificent. Her arousal scent is crisp and floral, and yet her taste is rich and sweet, and somehow warm. I did not know warm had a taste, but that is the word that comes to mind as I run my tongue along the seam of her pouty lips. Her mouth is small, but her lips are full and shaped like a heart when she smiles with her mouth closed. It is my favorite of her smiles. She has many, as I have learned over our short time together, and I like that one best.

She moans softly as my fingers tangle in her short spiky hair. Just a hint of a sound, barely audible, but enough to let me know she is in this just as much as I am. I feel the rough tip of her small tongue rub against my lips, and heat floods my core as I let her in. Jo's hands start as clenched fists in her lap, but eventually I feel one of them rest lightly on my shoulder while the other cups my cheek. Such a tender touch from such a powerful little witch.

It is clear she is nervous, but there is no reason for her to be. What Jo lacks in proficiency, she makes up for in intensity. The heat of her body pulls me in, making me dizzy with need. Her small hands grip me tighter, and I feel myself getting wetter by the moment. It is a frantic, chaotic desire that has me on the verge of tearing her beautiful dress to shreds while also respecting her need to go slowly. I wish to savor her taste for as long as she will let me.

Move her onto her back! my draxilio urges. *Shove your tongue between her thighs!*

It has been many *soliqs* since my body felt release without the use of devices or my hand, so my draxilio is quite eager for me to move things along with Jo. But for the first time in I cannot remember how long, I do not follow her command. I am far too focused on Jo's needs, and how to make her feel good.

Besides, this rush of emotions and this strange inkling to be patient with Jo is merely due to the length of time I have longed to seduce her. That is all. I shall go slowly, for now, because that is what she needs. But eventually, we will have sex, and my desire for her will wane as it has with everyone else once my needs are met. In the meantime, we will have a joyous time exploring each other's bodies.

According to our handlers, mates do not exist for us podlings. Niro has proven this to be inaccurate upon finding Kate, but he could be the lucky one among us. I am not counting on the rest of us finding mates.

When I suck on the tip of her tongue, Jo lets out a breathy little whimper that I wish I could capture in a jar and listen to it whenever I desire. I am certain it is a sound I shall never forget.

Her body trembles against me, then she suddenly jerks back with wide eyes. We apologize at the same time, then chuckle at our timing.

I decide to go first with my explanation for the apology. "I did not ask first if I may kiss you. For that, I am sorry, Jo."

"It is all right," Jo replies, shaking her head as if my apology was silly and unnecessary. "I am sorry that the kiss was not good. I…" she trails off. "I had not done that before."

"Ever?" I ask, astonished, mostly because the kiss was better than good. It was sensational. But I am also shocked because how has no one ever kissed this radiant pixie before? Is everyone on Trovilia a complete and utter fool?

Go to Trovilia! my draxilio shouts. *Ask them! Ask them why they did not notice this lovely creature!*

She seems to have forgotten the device our handlers attached to our hearts before sending us here from Sufoi. The device that will cause our hearts to stop the moment we breach Oluura's atmosphere, killing us instantly.

I have not forgotten! It would be a worthy sacrifice!

No, I send back. *No, it would not.*

"I do not understand. You have never been with another?" I ask Jo.

She tilts her head back as she thinks, a nervous gesture that I find adorable. "Well, I have had female pleasure mates before, although the last time I was with a female was centuries ago. Kissing was just never part of it."

I find this somewhat odd, but perhaps kissing for their kind is a new thing. I did not realize their race lived such long lives, and I certainly had not considered that Jo was older than me. Natural-born draxilios live seven hundred years, at least, and genetically modified draxilios live even longer. I had assumed we were the oldest race in the universe. Plus, the other members of the clan seem much younger than Jo. "What is the average age of a Trovilian?"

"Most Trovilians live past two centuries. Hexrins, though, live much longer. I am past my fifth century."

A gasp escapes me. "Truly? I am not even three hundred yet."

She giggles shyly, her small hand covering her mouth.

The intensity of my feelings paired with the revelation that Jo had never been kissed before has left me feeling unsettled. And the shouts from my draxilio do not help either. It is probably why the next words out of my mouth are: "Mek was not possessed. It was a fabrication to bring you here and seduce you."

CHAPTER 5

JO

*S*uppose I should be angry at Alu for lying about Mek's condition. While I am certainly not pleased to learn I have been tricked into coming to her cottage, anger is not one of the emotions I feel. There is frustration, there is also amusement, and most importantly, there is relief.

Truthfully, I would not know where to begin in order to free an ancient spirit from a jungle bird, so I am glad that is not a task I shall have to complete. There is a ritual I have done to free spirits from Trovilians, but never animals. The relief is also tied to how comfortable I feel here compared to Kayt and Nee-roh's caves. There is more space to practice my magic, and while I adore Kayt, it seemed as if she felt the need to constantly entertain me, which I found to be exhausting.

There is one question, however, I simply must ask. "Did you think I would decline an invitation to stay with you?"

Alu remains silent for a moment as she ponders this. "I suppose I did. Or, rather, I did not know how to tell you I wished to seduce you, other than saying the words in that very order." Her chin dips. "I have been told my boldness makes others uncomfortable."

I find Alu's blunt way of communicating quite refreshing. As a

Hexrin, I have the ability to tap into others' minds and hear their thoughts if I wish, but that is not something I would need to do with her. She is direct in a way I have not encountered with anyone. Other than Bruvix, perhaps, but his direct words are often just telling people to leave him alone.

What surprises me most about this lie is that Alu felt she needed to do it in the first place. As if there was a possibility that I would have no interest in spending time alone with her at her cottage. Who would refuse such an enticing offer?

"I am not mad," I finally tell her. "I am flattered."

Alu's eyes swirl with heat at my response.

"Besides, I left the clan to work on my craft. I must find a way to control my power before I return to my coven. So I am happy to stay and focus on that."

Her brow furrows as she tilts her head to the side. "Why must you control it? The power of a witch is an evolving thing, constantly growing, is it not?"

"That is true," I explain, "but I have inflicted pain upon members of the clan with the use of my power. It is my responsibility to ensure that never happens again." Although, perhaps it is less about controlling it and more about understanding it because the surge of energy I felt between my palms when I built the fire orb that hit Nalba was unlike anything I have conjured before.

"I was present during the battle against Bzzsil Chi," Alu says.

I nod. "Yes, I remember." As if I could forget the way she smiled at Bzzsil's henchman when he tried to attack her moments before she shifted into her draxilio and used her flame to melt the flesh off his bones. She was spectacular.

"I do not recall you causing anyone harm," she says, her tone taking on an intense, defensive edge. "That male Hexrin who pushed you is the one to blame for the pain Nalba suffered."

I sigh heavily. "Yes, Tibik is his name."

Alu's lips curl back in a snarl. "I do not like this Tibik. Why is he in charge of the coven? You should be leading them."

It is nice to hear this sentiment from the lips of another, especially

Alu's. I have felt alone in this belief for so long, and now I have Alu on my side.

Kayt is the only one who knows the truth: that my power is strong enough to claim the role of Prime Hexrin, and I am merely allowing Tibik to act as if the role is his. However, I do not like the ego Tibik has developed as of late. His approach to magic has been questionable at best, and dangerous at worst. He needs to be put in his place, but am I truly ready to take on the role of Prime? Do I even want it?

"I...I do not know if I am capable of leading a coven," I mutter quietly, finally voicing a fear that has burrowed deep into my mind and remained there for many years.

Alu throws her head back and laughs. "That is absurd."

She does not seem to understand. "I could have closed my palms when Tibik intervened, letting the orb dissipate," I say, referring to the battle with Bzzsil Chi. "I did not because the force of the orb was greater than anything I have ever felt. I was greedy, and I chased my power to defy Tibik."

"I do not see the problem," she says plainly.

"What if I become greedy with it again?" I ask, my voice dropping to a whisper. "What if I cannot control it? What if..." I begin, afraid to finish my thought, "I am as reckless as my coven thinks I am?"

Alu smiles widely, showing most, if not all, of her teeth. "Then it is good you are here." She slaps the cushion of the couch as she leaps to her feet. "What I hear from your mouth, Jo, is fear. That is all there is...an endless stream of thoughts rooted in fear."

"Well, yes," I say, knowing this to be true. I have spent enough time inside my head to know it is a fearful place.

"Who better to support you during this time than a formidable creature who is incapable of feeling fear?"

I suppose Alu has a point. What stands in my way is an emotion she has never felt. To be near her, to witness how she approaches each moment, could perhaps help me overcome this uncertainty I have about leading the coven.

"Me!" she shouts when I do not answer her rhetorical question. "It is me, Jo. I am the one who shall help you through this."

I chuckle at her need to clarify what I already knew. "You are right," I say, clearing my throat as I stand. "There is no better place for me to be than right here."

Alu claps her hands together, and I hear Mek squawking in protest from down the hall. She quiets her claps immediately, and in a whisper, she says, "This is wonderful! Oh, is there anything you need to practice your magic?"

"No, no," I assure her. "I shall find everything I need in nature." If I cannot find what I need from the surrounding land, I shall have to make it myself. It is a crucial rule in Hexrin magic.

"Very well," she says, "I am going to let my draxilio out for a long flight. Enjoy your magic practice."

Before I can take a step toward the front door, Alu wraps her hand around my wrist. She leans in close, and I shiver as her hot breath tickles my ear. "Also, I vow to not kiss you again unless you request otherwise."

My throat suddenly feels dry as the memory of our kiss takes over my mind. I can still feel her plump blue lips closing around the tip of my tongue. The feel of her bare skin on mine. A noise rips from my throat, not a word, but a strained, desperate sound, like, "Hnnh."

I do not like this vow she offers me. Fear is all I know. It is all I have known for centuries. If she does not continue to act on her impulses the way she does, fearlessly, will we never kiss again? "What if I want you to kiss me, but I am too afraid to ask?"

Alu's gaze drops from my eyes to my lips and back again. "Would a Prime Hexrin ask to be kissed? Or would they act on their desires?"

"Well, I suppose they would act on their desires," I begin, "but surely you are not suggesting I kiss you before asking if it is allowed. What if you do not want me to kiss you?"

She chuckles, shaking her head. Then her grip tightens on my wrist as she pulls me against her. "There will never come a time when I do not want you to kiss me, tiny witch. Trust me on that."

CHAPTER 6

JO

It is late into the morning by the time Alu returns home from her flight. I crane my head back to watch her circle above her cottage in her draxilio form before she gradually floats down to the ground. Her massive claws dig into the soil beneath her feet as she stretches her long, thick neck. Then she shakes her gigantic draxilio head, and the shake travels down her neck, into her chest, and ripples through the rest of her body. It reminds me of the way Stahn-lee the tr-gory pup shakes the muck out of his fur after he has been playing in a puddle.

Alu steals my breath when she is in this form. It still mystifies me that this terrifying creature who sits before me—with her many sharp teeth and black spikes running down her back—who is twice the size of the cottage, shares a mind with the uniquely brilliant and beautiful female who kissed me only hours prior.

My eyes travel down the shimmering blue scales of her draxilio body, and I notice there is something clutched inside her back left claw. She turns it over, and dozens of round pink fruits spill onto the ground. A heartbeat later, Alu shifts into her flightless form and starts gathering the fruit in her arms with an excited look on her face.

"Come help me carry these," she says. I race to her side and start tucking them into my arms.

It takes three trips to bring all of them inside. "What are they?" I ask, turning one over in my hand.

"I call them juicy sour balls," she says with a shrug, as she bites through the tough skin. The pale pink juice drips down her chin and runs down her chest, leaving a wet mark in the center of her olive-green top that wraps around her breasts and ribs. The bottom half of her stomach is bared, and my gaze lingers on the muscles that contract with each breath she takes.

I still do not understand the mechanics of the Sufoian device implanted in Alu's arm that removes her clothes upon shifting into her draxilio, and puts them back on when she returns to her flightless form, but I am quite amazed by it.

"Try one," she urges, gesturing to the fruit I am still holding. Without knowing much about this fruit other than what Alu calls it, I am hesitant to bite into it. But as I watch Alu continue to sink her teeth into hers, sucking and licking the juices that spill forth, well, I am losing interest in eating altogether. I am also reminded that this is a small example of how fear guides my choices.

It is fruit. There is nothing dangerous about it. I should not be so hesitant to take a bite.

Closing my eyes, I dive in, fangs first, and I am overwhelmed as the sour, but tasty liquid of the juicy sour ball floods my tongue. "Mmm," I mumble with my mouth full.

"Mmm-hmm," Alu replies encouragingly, deep into her second juicy sour ball.

We eat several of these fruits, quietly munching side by side in Alu's eating room. The juice stains our clothes completely by the time we are finished.

"Oh no!" Alu cries as she takes in the state of my dress. "Wait here. I shall get something for you to wear, so we may wash this."

I wait in the eating room, my hands sticky from the juice and my belly full of fruit. It was not a balanced meal by any means, but it was certainly delicious.

Alu returns moments later with clothing draped over her arm; without putting our sticky fingers on the garments, she transfers the clothes to my arm. "The washroom is at the end of the hall on the left."

I lift the arm that is holding the clothing. "Thank you for these."

Alu's washroom is quite roomy, with sparkling white tiles on the walls and floor, a waste box in the far corner, two sinks, and a large wash box that the entire coven could fit into. Once I am inside the wash box, the smell of Alu's soap causes me to moan as I work it into my mane and massage my scalp. The dominant scent is crisp and fresh like the Trovilian sea, with just a hint of sweetness.

I use one of Alu's giant towels to dry off and put on her clothes. The black sleeveless shirt is loose in the chest area, which is to be expected, as my breasts are much smaller than hers. The pants, however, are far too big, but luckily Alu put a thin belt made of rope in here, and it is strong enough to hold my pants up when I secure it around my waist. I roll the cuffs of the pants up to my shins and tuck them into the tops of my boots, and then make my way out to the main room.

Alu smiles brightly when she sees me. "You look lovely."

I can feel my cheeks heat as her gaze drifts down my body. "Thank you," I reply, my tone quiet.

She says she is going to check on Mek in his room, and I head outside to continue practicing my magic. Beginning with the exercises I learned at the Hexrin academy, I go through each, and then eventually move on to the moderate and more advanced spells. I find them all to be incredibly easy, and I start to wonder why I am behaving as if I have forgotten everything I have learned. There is no reason for me to treat this as a re-education of basic craft.

Knowing I have the space to push my boundaries, and that no one shall be hurt in the process, I start working with orbs. I am able to manipulate the elements in nature and capture them in an orb between my hands, so that is what I do.

Starting with air, I spread my fingers wide while holding my hands shoulder-width apart. Closing my eyes, I listen to the sound of the wind moving through the trees, lifting leaves off the ground, and kicking around minuscule bits of dust and dirt from various surfaces. Then, slowly, I move my hands closer together as I envision trapping the wind inside the orb. It whistles as I draw it toward me, getting louder with each bit of distance I remove between my hands.

I feel the familiar flicker of excitement the moment the wind picks up inside the orb, whipping around in a frenzy as I hold it in place. This is the feeling that terrifies me. Bending nature to my will is an acknowledgment of the strength of my power. A voice inside my head shouts for me to let go, to release the wind to its natural state, as I have no right to manipulate the weather. But I ignore the voice, just as I think Alu would if she had the voice of fear inside her head. She would hold tight to see what comes of this.

Continuing to close the distance between my hands becomes a strenuous act, and I grit my teeth as I struggle to push against the force of the power inside the orb that is desperate to break free. Every muscle in my body is rigid as I keep my gaze locked on the orb.

I am moments from reaching the orb's full strength. I can feel it. Soon I shall turn my palms outward and up, shooting the orb into the sky and releasing the wind from the ball I trapped it in.

Before I can, a scream echoes through the jungle, coming from the cliffs on the other side of the cottage.

Alu. She is hurt.

Letting the orb fizzle between my hands, I race through the front entrance and out the side door from the eating room to the balcony and notice her draxilio is flying up from the pool, awkwardly flapping her left wing. She shifts into her flightless form as soon as she reaches the balcony and collapses just outside the door in a heap of limbs.

"Alu! What happened?" I ask frantically as I crouch at her side. Her right arm is cut just above her elbow, and blood is covering part of the intricate black tattoo that swirls from her shoulder down to her wrist.

"*Rekko tuv,*" she mutters under her breath as she gets to her feet. *Stupid rock.* "I was swinging from the ropes into the water, but as I reached for one, I missed and landed against a rock."

"It looks serious," I say, as I pull the towel draped over the balcony and press it against her wound.

"No," she says, waving a dismissive hand, "it shall be fine. I heal quickly."

I wish I had the power to heal others, but that is not magic I possess. I have no idea how to help Alu right now, and that guts me. What if her injury was worse than this?

"Why do you swing on the ropes at all?" I ask as she wraps the towel around her bicep and pins it between her arm and her ribs.

She tilts her head to the side as her brow lifts. "Why would I not swing on the ropes?" she asks. When I do not answer her question, she adds, "It is fun."

"But look at what has occurred!" I shout, surprising myself with the volume of my voice. "It seems too dangerous an activity. You should not do it anymore."

Alu chuckles. "Jobaki, I am not going to stop doing something I enjoy because it did not go perfectly one time."

"It could have been worse, Alu," I explain. I do not understand why I am not getting through to her. Does she not see the risks involved? "What if your head hits that rock instead of your arm?"

She shrugs at my words then turns on her heel as she goes inside. Over her shoulder, she says, "It would hurt, but I would be fine."

I find I am somewhat stung by her casual reaction to her injury. While draxilios live a very long time and are hard to kill, and she is immune to fear, I still do not want to see Alu in pain, even if that pain is minimal. The panic I felt at seeing blood running down her arm was almost debilitating.

Perhaps I am growing too attached to my host, and I know it is because we kissed. It is also because there is more I wish to do with her than kiss, and I have a feeling we will reach that place soon. But I must be careful with my heart. I cannot allow it to beat for Alu, as I am not able to take a mate.

We are too different, anyway. How would a relationship between us work? She would be making wild, ill-advised choices, and I would be constantly petrified that one of those choices would lead to her death. I cannot live that way.

There is too much for me to focus on at the moment. I should not be allowing thoughts of Alu becoming my inara to keep me from working on my magic. I wince at the sight of Alu's blood on the edge of the balcony and grab another towel from the stack by the door to remove it. Once I am finished, I let my gaze wander over the cliffs beneath Alu's home as the steady rush of the waterfall fills my ears. I realize I have yet to explore this side of Alu's property.

Glancing back at the cottage, I see Alu tending to her wound in the main room. I feel unsettled by the strength of my worries for her well-being. Perhaps this is a good time to take a walk and hope my nerves settle a bit.

Climbing over the land-facing side of the balcony, my boots sink into the soft soil, and I follow the narrow dirt path that leads away from the waterfall and deeper into the jungle. With my smaller frame, it is easy to duck beneath low branches and sidestep wide, prickly bushes, but eventually, the trail ends, and the trees become denser. I suppose I could turn around and return to the house, but I might find some supplies out here to make a fresh herb bundle for my spells.

I wiggle my way between two close-together trees, and as soon as my boot hits the ground, a dark, thick energy wraps around me and sends me to my knees. A pained moan escapes me as I press against the sides of my head, trying to push the energy away, but it is impossible. I do not know what this is, or where it is coming from, but it is incredibly strong, and far too close to Alu's cottage for my liking.

Suddenly, blurred images flash through my mind. I see dirt and blood flying through the air as swords clash. The pounding of a multitude of feet race across the soil as a combination of rage and excitement pumps through the creatures' veins.

Crawling in the direction of home, I find my way out of the ominous cloud and the images fade. My hands shake as I pull myself to my feet and stumble down the narrow dirt trail. Part of me wishes to run inside and warn Alu of this mysterious darkness, but then I remember her injury and how she reacted to it. If I reveal this to her, she will want to investigate it, and the absence of fear will put her in danger by allowing her curiosity to take the lead when caution should be guiding her instead. No, I cannot share this with her. Not yet.

Not until I determine what it is and how to keep her safe from it.

CHAPTER 7

ALU

Jo is quiet after she returns from practicing her magic, and she remains that way through dinner. I do not know what troubles her, but I find that her shift in mood is troubling *me*. And how can she stand to remain this quiet, even when she is upset? When it is only Mek and I here, I am always speaking to him. He talks back, and though I do not speak bird, I like the way he engages with me.

"Did you not enjoy the way I prepared the vegetables?" I ask, trying to uncover the root cause of her silence.

She chuckles softly. "No, I loved it. I had no idea your method of cooking vegetables consisted of shifting into your draxilio and blowing fire onto them."

I nod proudly. "I did not see the need to install a separate component onto my food dispenser to cook the food when that is something I can do in my other form simply by breathing."

"Quite sensible of you," Jo replies, taking a long sip of tibbi. If that is not what is bothering her, then what is?

"Did you struggle with your magic today?" I ask. It saddens me that she feels disconnected from such an integral part of who she is. To be disconnected from my draxilio would be utterly devastating.

My draxilio chooses this moment to remind me of just how connected we are. *Kiss her! Make her feel better!*

I ignore her suggestions, as I do not feel they would be well received. But I do place my hand on top of Jo's to show her I am empathetic to her predicament. "You can share your struggles with me. I cannot help you solve Hexrin problems, but I am happy to listen."

Warmth fills her golden eyes as she wraps her small fingers around mine. "Thank you," she says, giving my hand a squeeze. "Practicing my magic is going well so far. I think being able to do it here is helping."

I return her kind smile. "That is good."

We clean the dishes together and spend the rest of the evening chatting on the couch in the main room. I walk her to her room after she yawns thrice in a row, hoping she will kiss me, or at least ask if I want her to. She does neither, and my face falls the moment she closes the door.

Why did I vow to not kiss her again until she requests it? She is too shy to do such things. I shall be waiting a century before I am able to seduce her. A growl rumbles low in my chest as I undress and climb into bed.

Hours pass and the growl in my throat remains as I replay the events of the day in my head. Eventually, I come to the realization that Jo's mood changed after I hurt myself. Though I do not understand why she would have any lingering frustration. I am well. The gash on my arm stings, but it is a dull pain that is easy to ignore. It shall be gone by tomorrow night.

As I ponder ways to make her feel better about my mishap, I hear a light scratching sound coming from down the hall. Mek is in his room with the door shut, so it cannot be him, and it does not sound like a noise that could be tied to Jo fetching herself a drink of water in the middle of the night either. This is an inconsistent scratching that does not cease.

That means there is a predator outside trying to get in. Or a predator that has already gotten inside.

I make my steps light and quick as I step out of my room and toward the noise. Jo's door is closed, and I hope she is still fast asleep. I shall handle this intruder swiftly to ensure her slumber is not interrupted.

The main room is empty, and the deeper I step into the house, the clearer the scratching sound becomes. Whatever it is, they are trying to enter through the side door that opens onto the balcony. It is too small an area for me to shift into my draxilio and handle the intruder properly, but even in this form, I am not concerned about defeating them.

The light in the eating room turns on automatically once I enter, and it illuminates the balcony enough to reveal the source of the scratching. It is a short, portly creature with black and brown scales covering its narrow-pointed head, neck, and wide torso, and long yellow feathers on its back and legs. The creature's arms are thin and weak looking, ending in two claws on each hand. It waddles in a circle on the balcony, sniffing and clawing at a few scattered leaves.

Perhaps it is hungry? Yes, that is it. This creature must be in search of food, and since I have picked the surrounding trees and bushes clean, it is struggling to find something to fill its belly. That is easily rectified. Pulling a juicy sour ball from the cold box, I carefully open the door to the balcony and step outside with the fruit placed in my open palm.

"Here," I say to the creature, holding the fruit higher. "Food."

Its eyes are pitch black with vertical slits and no pupils. The creature remains still as it blinks at me. I assume this means it cannot understand what I am offering, so I take a step closer and repeat, "Food."

"Alu! What are you doing?" Jo whispers from inside the door. "Come back inside."

Turning to face her, I explain, "Do not worry. It is just hungry. I am gi—"

My words are cut off as the creature shoves me from behind. I land hard on my knees, and the juicy sour ball goes flying over the edge of the balcony into the water below. The creature hisses as it watches the fruit's descent. After the splash of it landing in the water, the creature's posture looks aggressive as it faces me. It seems to grow in height as an ominous clicking sound emanates from its throat between hisses.

I am not worried, however, because a swift kick into the creature's stomach will get it to back off. I just need enough space to get the leverage required for the kick. Slowly crawling backward on my elbows, I make soft soothing noises in an attempt to confuse it into thinking I am afraid.

"Alu!" Jo calls. Her voice is still hushed, but there is greater urgency in it now. "Get back in here right now!"

Answering her and explaining my plan would give the creature enough time to attack, which I do not want. It is best to ignore Jo momentarily so I may handle this beast the way I need.

Raising its clenched fists above its head, the feathered reptilian slams them onto the wood floor of my balcony, busting two large holes in it that I will need to repair. I am not skilled at home repair, so I find this new development quite frustrating.

The creature takes a step closer and raises its fists again, and just as I am bringing my foot back, Jo bursts through the door. "No!" she screams as she places her small body between me and the creature. Before I can push her out of harm's way, she lifts her palms in front of her heart and a bright orange orb appears between them. Then she thrusts her upper body forward as she turns her palms, shooting the orb into the creature's chest.

The creature lets out a screeching cry as its body is thrown from the balcony high into the air, only beginning its descent toward the ground when it's well over the other side of the waterfall.

I scramble to my feet and watch in awe as Jo remains locked in her strong, defiant stance. Grabbing her shoulders, I turn her around until she is facing me. "That was superb, Jo! Brilliant work!"

Her breathing turns into rapid pants as she stares at me. "Brilliant?" she says as tears fill her eyes, and her cheeks turn a darker shade of gold. "Brilliant?" she repeats, this time in a shout. "You thought that was brilliant? That thing could have killed you!"

I suppose it did have the strength to put up a solid fight, but no, there is no way that creature could have killed me. I am far too strong. "That is not true. I was in no danger."

"You do not know that for certain!" she yells, the tears spilling onto her smooth cheeks. "How can you be so careless?"

Careless? "How was I being careless? I thought it was hungry, so I offered it food."

She paces around the small part of the balcony that was not damaged by the creature's fists. "What if something had happened to you?" Then she steps in front of me, her eyes boring into mine. "What if that beast had…" she swallows, her entire body trembling, "had…"

Instead of finishing her thought, she grabs me by the waist and pulls me against her body as her lips crash into mine. At first, I am too stunned to respond. This tiny, timid sorceress is holding me against her body with the strength of a hundred draxilios, her firm, yet soft mouth hot and desperate as it seizes mine.

When I feel her tongue stroke against my bottom lip, it is as if my body finally awakens, and I shove my hands into her short cropped hair, as my tongue darts into her mouth, exploring, tasting, and savoring. I do not need to reach a hand between my thighs to know I am soaked. Just having Jobaki in my home has kept me in a constant state of arousal.

She moans, and it is a needy, aching sound that makes me want to lift her in my arms, throw her onto the couch, and make her come over and over and over until her body can take no more.

Splendid idea! my draxilio purrs. *Do that!*

She is right. It is a splendid idea.

Jo lets out a surprised squeal as I lift her in my arms and carry her inside, my lips returning to hers immediately. I do not need to open my eyes to know where I am taking her. When my shin brushes against the lantern at the top of the stairs, I take two steps to the right and down two more until we are in the sunken seating area that fills the center of the main room.

She whimpers softly the moment my lips leave hers, but then her eyes widen with shock as I toss her into the air. The moment she lands on the soft cushions, she giggles, and it lights up her entire face. The breath leaves my body entirely at the sight of her like this—free of worries, unburdened by responsibilities to her coven, and excited about the unknown that lies ahead.

I am willing to bet that she has only felt this way a handful of times in her very long life, and I find that heartbreaking. It seems as if giving her more of these moments is now my main purpose.

Though, perhaps that is a sentiment too strong for what is between the two of us. At the very least, I shall give her more of these moments tonight.

CHAPTER 8

JO

Alu undresses me slowly, her lips leaving a hot trail over my skin. She is branding me as hers, and I am stunned by how much I want that too. It has been so long since I have done this with another that I can barely remember how it feels or what I am supposed to do. No matter what comes of this, Alu will leave me forever changed, because, while I may not remember past lovers, I am certain I will not forget her.

My breaths turn heavy the moment she tosses my pants behind her, leaving me completely naked and spread before her. She shoots me a wicked grin as she sinks to her knees, and her gray eyes remain locked on mine as she crawls toward me, only stopping when her hot breath tickles my inner thigh.

Her gaze drops to my cunt just before she strokes the length of my seam with her finger. I suck in a breath as I watch her bring that finger to her mouth, and her tongue swirls around it.

"Mmm," she moans, her eyes falling closed. Then she leans in and presses slow, soft kisses to my thighs and across the lower part of my stomach, little flicks of her tongue at the end of each one. She continues this pattern as her mouth gets closer to my core.

I throw my head back against the cushion, impatient and frustrated by her teasing. She chuckles upon seeing this, and after three more kisses to my belly, she flattens her tongue against my soaked folds and drags it upward. Alu laps at my center, sucking on the lips of my cunt in between long, electrifying strokes of her tongue.

Brushing the long strands of her mane off her face, I watch as her tongue disappears inside my body, and the muscles of my cunt instantly contract and flex around her. My entire body begins to shake, and briefly, I wonder if I am close to coming already. Surely, that cannot be. It is far too soon for that despite the centuries that have passed between the last time I experienced this and now.

When Alu groans, I realize it is not me at all. It is her. Specifically, her tongue. It is vibrating inside me.

I gasp at the realization as my hands wrap around her thick, proud horns. "I did not know you c-could do that."

She groans again, a hint of laughter in the sound, as she uses her tongue to explore every depth and crevice of my cunt. I feel the pulsing of my *k'billita* as her tongue caresses the swollen twin buds deep within me, and my back arches so high that I practically lift off the couch.

"Yes," I whimper, my claws sinking into the pillows on either side of me. "Yes. Yes."

It feels as if her tongue is everywhere, stroking and sucking on each speck of my bare skin, and *everywhere* is precisely where I want her.

She presses her hands against my thighs, exposing more of me to her as she dives deeper, reaching places inside I did not know were even there. I cry out as my hands go to my breasts. I squeeze and pinch my nipples as my muscles tighten from my head to my toes. Each flutter of my cunt brings me closer to release as my walls flex against her vibrating tongue.

My hips buck against her mouth, first in a steady rhythm, then erratically as the tip of her tongue flicks against each of my k'billita, back and forth, back and forth, until I am screaming and trying to climb out of my own skin.

I expect Alu to pull out of me, at least to require a break to breathe, but she does not. She continues her assault on my cunt until I am flying over the edge, my legs kicking into the air and my entire body quaking with the force of my orgasm.

My limbs are boneless as I lie there, trying to catch my breath. Alu climbs up my body and props herself on her elbow at my side. I feel my heart stop as she tenderly strokes a finger along my cheek, jawline, and down my neck.

"Does any other part of you vibrate?" I ask once I finally come down.

"No," she says with a half-giggle. "Our tongues do not vibrate naturally. It was a procedure I had done on Sufoi."

"Oh," I reply, surprised by the admission. "Why would you want that done?"

"Why do you think?" she asks, rhetorically.

I laugh at how silly my question was. While the memories of my previous orgasm with a partner are hazy, I am certain I have never had one as good as that. Alu's vibrating tongue was a magnificent surprise. "Of course," I eventually reply.

At some point, we both fall asleep on the couch. I am awakened when Alu carries me to her bedroom and climbs into bed beside me, but it takes only a moment to drift into a deep slumber once more.

I awaken to find the spot beside me in bed completely empty, so I grab one of Alu's shirts from off the floor and throw it over my head before I wander down the hall in search of her. It is far earlier than I care to be awake, with the sun still low in the sky. But when I find Alu sitting in the doorway to the balcony, Mek on her shoulder as she feeds him small berries, I am thrilled I was not asleep to miss this.

She does not notice my presence, as her back is turned, and so I continue to watch her. She asks Mek how he slept the previous eve and if he thought she could have bested the reptilian creature that broke through the floor of the balcony, and he lets out a low cooing sound between berries.

"I agree," she says to him. "This balcony is too dangerous to stand on. Though I do not know how I am going to fix it."

The sight of her like this, calm and still, but with her uniquely curious spirit, makes me think she would seamlessly fit into the clan. I think the coven would even grow to like her. Most of the time, Alu is quite loud. It is not just in the volume of her voice, but in everything she does.

Her lack of fear seems directly connected to her clumsiness, as the fear of repercussions the rest of us feel after making a mess or breaking something is simply not there. She is not afraid of how she is perceived by others, either, which is a quality I am envious of, but also contributes to her inability to detect common social cues.

These little parts of her personality are not flaws, and they do not define who she is, because at her core, Alu is essentially an open beating heart who happens to take the form of a beautiful female. They make me like her more than I did, which was already quite a bit.

But that is me.

It is not the clan, and it is not the coven. I worry that they will find her presence obtrusive, and I worry even more that her feelings will be hurt by the way she is treated. I do not want that, but I also cannot stay here forever. I must return to my coven eventually. The question is, will Alu go with me? Or at least visit me occasionally, so that we may continue this…whatever this is between us?

Quietly, I back away from Alu and Mek, and grab my boots by the front door before I step outside. I am curious to see if the dark energy I felt the previous day remains, and if there is anything I can do to clear it.

This time, I approach with caution once I reach the end of the narrow dirt path. I pick up a long, thin twig from the ground and hold it out in front of me as I continue forward. The moment the tip of the stick breaches the surface, something races up the length of the wood and sends a painful spark into my palm. I drop the stick instinctively and take a step back to reassess.

Instead of entering it, which the source of this energy clearly does not want me to do, I close my eyes and focus on bringing it to me. Keeping my feet planted, I turn my palms toward the sky as I envision pulling a corner of that energy toward me. I need just a sliver of it to get a sense of what it is and what it wants.

After several moments of this, the dark energy does not move. While my mind screams at me to turn back and give up this pointless pursuit, I find I am far too intrigued to walk away. If this were a cluster of dark energy in a far corner of Oluura that no one in our clan would ever cross, I would be inclined to leave it be. But this is right next to Alu's home. I cannot just leave it as it is. For her safety, I must learn more.

Since I cannot bring it to me, I step forward once again. Last time, I felt like I was drowning in it while enveloped in the cluster. This time, however, it is only when I stick a foot inside that I am knocked to the ground. The energy here…it has strengthened. How can that be?

There is a whisper in the air as the energy fills my lungs. I cannot understand the words, as it is a language I am not familiar with, but it sounds as if it is saying *seccoossvun.*

A groan releases from my throat as I flop onto my belly and crawl away. My palms are covered in scrapes and my head is pounding, but eventually, I break free. When I turn around, I am shocked to discover the short distance I traveled from where the cluster of dark energy begins, and where I am now. It felt like I was crawling through mud, a slow, miserable slog to escape its clutches. Something inside of it did not want me to leave. It wanted to keep me there.

"Jo?" I hear Alu call out from the front of the cottage. I rub my palms against my tunic, trying to clear away the dirt as I stumble back toward her.

"Morivikka," I say, offering the standard Trovilian greeting once I emerge from the dirt path. "You called for me?"

Her brow furrows as she looks at the direction from which I came, then back to me, then back down the path once again. "Where were you?"

"Oh, I was collecting some twigs to make a sigil," I lie.

It is enough to convince her, though, because she smiles brightly. "Kate sent a comm on the screen pad. She wishes to speak with you."

I follow her into the house, relieved she did not question me further when I clearly returned without a single twig in hand. Alu gives me her screen pad, and I take it into the spare bedroom. I send a comm back to Kayt and a moment later, her pale, freckled face appears.

"Jo!" she shouts excitedly. "I miss you. How's your stay been? Is Alu being a good host?"

"Yes, yes," I reply with an amused tone. Kayt has grown protective of me during our friendship. It is nice knowing she cares so much for me. "I am having a splendid time. I have been working on my magic here, strengthening my focus, and it is going well."

She must see something in my expression, or perhaps the darkening of my cheeks, because she leans in close to the screen pad and gives me a discerning look. "Are you two hooking up?"

"Err, I do not understand," I reply. Her words have me envisioning a steel hook being pulled into the sky, but that does not seem right.

She rolls her eyes. "Sorry, I meant…having sex, or engaging in the intimate acts that lead up to sex."

It is not that I do not trust Kayt, I just do not know if this is something Alu wants her to know, so after a long pause—too long, probably—I say, "No, we are no—"

"You are," she replies, her mouth hanging open.

That is when I give up trying to keep it a secret. Sighing, I say, "Well, yes, we have. But Kayt," I add, taking a deep breath, "there is something I must ask you."

She nods. "Shoot."

"How long did it take the clan to accept Niro, and his," I am not sure how to express this, "unique ways?"

"Mmm-hmm," she replies, "you're worried the clan won't like Alu. Is that it?"

For a human, Kayt is quite sharp. In my time away from her, it seems I have forgotten that. "Yes," I whisper, hoping Alu is not outside the door listening in. "I worry that some may not understand the ways in which she is different, and they will not treat her with the kindness she deserves."

Kayt chews on the inside of her cheek as she ponders this. "Alu is a bit of an outdoor cat."

"What is *cat?* This is a creature from your planet?"

"Yeah," she says with a laugh. "But it's an expression for when you're describing someone who isn't the most comfortable or charismatic in social settings. And I see what you mean about how others might treat her, but I find her to be incredibly charismatic, and without fear, she seems perfectly comfortable in the social settings I've seen her in. So I don't think you have to worry too much."

"You think so?" I ask, hoping she is right. The last thing I want is for Alu to encounter any rudeness from the clan, or, more specifically, the coven, because she is different.

"I mean, she's a fucking dragon who lacks fear," Kayt says with a proud smile. "That's the kind of person you want on your side. The clan would be lucky to be graced with her presence on a consistent basis."

She is right. Our clan needs Alu more than Alu needs us.

Kayt says she misses me a few more times before we disconnect the comm. I return to the main room with a sense of relief loosening my shoulders.

When I hand the screen pad back to Alu, she asks, "Was Niro on the comm?"

I find this to be an odd question. "No, it was just Kayt."

"Oh," she replies, her face falling slightly.

"Why do you ask?"

She is silent at first as she runs a claw along her chin. "My brothers do not think I am smart," she blurts. "I wondered if he got on the comm to tell you that."

"That you are not smart? Why would he say such a thing? How could he *think* such a thing?"

"Because I do not have a normal mind," she says plainly as if her statement and a lack of intelligence are inevitably linked.

"And? Neither do they." I ask. "That does not mean you are not smart. It just means your thoughts form in a different pattern than others." I did not expect to feel a deep, visceral rage toward Nee-roh, but it grows within the depths of my belly at this very moment for making Alu think such things.

Alu shrugs, as if not convinced that I speak the truth. Suddenly, it becomes my mission to not only protect Alu from harm, but also judgment and cruelty from others, even her own brothers, no matter the cost.

CHAPTER 9

ALU

It is becoming increasingly clear to me that sex is not the only thing I want from Jo. My original goal was to bring her to my home, seduce her, and then perhaps I would be able to stop thinking about her day and night. Eventually, she would leave, and this blinding desire I feel for her would cease.

That has not been my experience, however.

Even now, as we sit on the couch and enjoy a late afternoon snack of tibbi and *xid* candies, I am aware of her every movement, her every breath. My skin grows hot whenever her hand is near mine. We do not even have to touch for me to be overcome with need for her. I have become utterly obsessed with this tiny witch.

And when I made her come with my tongue last night, it was enough for me. Knowing I was able to bring her to release and had the honor of watching her face twist into an expression of blissful agony was incredibly fulfilling. I cannot remember a previous sexual encounter that I considered satisfying if I did not come.

While I long to have her hands and mouth all over my body, she has not had a pleasure mate in quite some time. I will not rush her. Her comfort is more important to me than anything else.

It is a vexing situation indeed. I am not used to focusing so intensely on another's emotions. It is usually just Mek here, and we are both fiercely independent creatures who occupy the same space. But with the addition of Jobaki, it feels as if the three of us are becoming a unit. This morning, he followed her outside to where she practiced her magic and remained perched on a nearby tree stump, watching her intently until she came in for some water.

Even now, his claws are wrapped around the brass edge of the table as he watches us enjoy our snack, and he is not trying to steal any of the xid candies, which is very unlike him. Instead, he waits patiently for Jo to give him one, and he gently pulls it from her grasp with the tip of his beak before tossing it up and catching it in his mouth.

Jo giggles every time, her nose scrunching up as she watches him, and my heart thunders inside my chest. And her scent…it is every-where, and it is intoxicating.

"Will you resume practicing your magic for the rest of the day?" I ask, eager to shift my attention to mundane topics instead of envi-sioning Jo with her legs thrown over my shoulders and my tongue swirling deep inside her cunt.

"Actually, yes, there's something new I'd like to try," she says, her eyes sparkling with mischief.

"How exciting," I reply, relieved she is able to find joy in using her powers once again. When she was at Kate and Niro's, she seemed so burdened and worn down. "Can I assist in this new sorcery?"

Her voice lowers to a rough, raspy sound. "You can, yes." Then she rises to her feet and walks toward my bedroom. She says nothing more, just looks at me coyly over her shoulder, and I am powerless to do anything but follow, my stomach fluttering in anticipation.

She closes the door behind me once we are inside the room, and I hear Mek cawing in protest outside the door. He will get bored waiting for us to return and fly off somewhere for the rest of the day. I am not worried about him.

Right now, there is nothing more important than Jo, and her heavy-lidded gaze as she takes my hand and guides me to the bed. She steps between my legs and looks up at me hesitantly. I know what she is thinking.

"You have my consent," I tell her. *Touch me however you wish,* I want to yell, *Just touch me! Now!* because that is how desperate I am to feel her skin against mine, but she is nervous at this moment, and I do not wish to frighten her.

I watch her throat work as she swallows, her eyes pinched closed, as if willing herself to make the first move.

Then her lips brush against mine—the lightest, tiniest caress, followed by a guttural moan as she pulls my head down and kisses me again, harder this time. Her hands become frantic as they roam freely over my clothes, stopping to squeeze my breasts and then my ass. I thrust my tongue between her lips, and she meets me with matching fervor as they tangle around each other while we claw at each other's clothes.

When her hand dips beneath the hem of my top and she rolls my hardened nipples between her fingers, my lips freeze and a whimper escapes me, my body already writhing against her. I rip the shirt over my head and toss it behind me. My pants come off next. Jo follows my lead, and within moments, we are both naked.

"You are so beautiful," I whisper, my chest squeezing at the sight of her smooth, golden skin. She is so petite, yet so powerful. Her nipples are a darker gold, matching the glistening lips of her cunt.

"Lie down for me," she commands in a soft, yet authoritative voice. "On your back."

I do as she says, settling in the center of the bed. The bed dips as she crawls up my body and settles herself between my legs. She holds herself above me on the bed and drops her head, her lips hovering above mine. I lift my neck to meet her, but she turns at the last moment, pressing a kiss to my neck instead.

A soft chuckle escapes me at her teasing ways.

She continues kissing a trail down my throat, licking and sucking as she goes, and I revel in the feel of her against me, the friction between our bodies making every nerve inside me come alive. I have waited so patiently for this and she has me teetering on the edge already.

Her lips close around my nipple and I scream, my back arching off the bed as my body surrenders. "Sensitive," I mutter, my breath shallow and panting as her fang brushes against the hardened tip of my breast before she pays the same attention to the other.

"Mmm," she moans against my breast, then releases my nipple with a pop. "So responsive." She is right. My nipples have always been incredibly sensitive. I often reach orgasm from just focused stimulation there.

My chest rises and falls rapidly as she runs her tongue all over my breasts, tasting and suckling. She does not miss a speck of bare skin. I grab onto the pillows behind me, needing something to hold onto as Jo's mouth moves down the center of my chest and then lower until her breath fans the swollen lips of my cunt.

"I am going to try my magic now," she says, reminding me of her earlier promise. I had forgotten it entirely the moment her lips touched mine.

I nod and lift my head to look down at her. She holds my gaze as her head dips, and she presses a soft kiss to my folds. Jo does this a few more times before I feel her tongue dart between my lips and stroke into my center, rubbing along the width of my *avuno,* the three throbbing bundles of nerves that line the depths of my inner walls.

Then…

Searing, brutal pleasure rips down my spine as my mouth falls open in a silent scream. It feels as if I am hurtling through space in a tight ball of flame. "Yes, Jo! Ohhhh," I cry out, and when I open my eyes, I notice a subtle pink glow rising from each of my nipples, down my chest and stomach—everywhere she put her lips on my body.

When she removes her tongue from the depths of my core, I whimper at the loss, but with a snap of her fingers, the glowing pink brightens, and I feel her mouth as if it's everywhere, all at once.

She kneels next to my head and holds out her hand. As soon as I take it, everything intensifies, and I lose all sense of where I am, or even who I am. All I know is that it feels like there are a dozen sets of plump lips kissing my nipples and cunt, and it is such an overwhelming sensation that I cannot breathe.

"Hold on tight, Alu," Jo whispers next to my ear. "The best is yet to come."

When she begins chanting under her breath, I tighten my grip on her hand. My skin starts to buzz as I am lifted off the bed, the glowing pink intensifying the higher Jo takes me. I feel my thighs start to shake as the magical mouths all over my body quicken their pace, their firm lips providing just the right amount of friction to unravel me.

Suddenly, Jo's body is curled against my side, both of us levitating as she presses soft kisses against my hair. "It is too much," I moan, through gritted teeth. "F-feel too much."

"You wish for me to stop?" she asks, running her nose along my jawline.

Well, no, I certainly do not want that. I want everything she has to give. I just do not know if my body can take it. However, there is only one way to find out.

"More," I reply, though it comes out as a low growl.

She whispers something I cannot understand, and with a sweep of her hand above my body, I come. I come and I come and I come. Like a ship crashing at the base of my spine, electric, searing heat shoots through my limbs and out through my fingers as my body bucks. Jo remains at my side, whispering sweet words of encouragement into my ear as she brushes the hair off my face.

I do not know how long this continues, but eventually, Jo covers me with a blanket, and I realize we are no longer levitating.

"That was…"

It was so incredible that I do not even have the words to finish the thought.

Jo seems to register this and chuckles softly. "I am glad I made you feel as good as you made me feel."

"No," I protest with a scoff. "I am certain the orgasm I gave you was nothing like the one you gave me."

She puts her hands behind her head, and her thighs part. "Then I suppose you have work to do."

I roll our bodies until she is on top of me, then I reach beneath her arms and lift, moving her into position. Once she is kneeling above my mouth, I spread the lips of her cunt, and smile up at her. "You best hold on then, tiny witch."

CHAPTER 10

JO

only get a fraction of the sleep I normally get, but I cannot complain. Alu has given me so many orgasms that I have lost count. I feel more rested and refreshed than I have felt in centuries.

We seem incapable of putting any amount of space between our bodies. Each time it occurs, by one of us moving or shifting in bed, we come together again, even if it is just our feet rubbing against each other. Our bodies are magnetic, and the pull between us feels as natural as breathing.

My only grievance is that we wasted so much time apart, when all along, we could have been doing this.

"Mmm," she moans, her voice dry and raspy from sleep. "Come here." She pulls me against her chest, and I feel her nipples harden against my bare back. Her hand dips between my thighs as she kisses along my neck, and I suck in a breath when her long, delicate fingers slip inside me.

"I want you to do something for me," she whispers, her fangs scraping along the skin beneath my ear.

"Mmm?" I moan, unable to reply articulately.

"Focus on what you want as I touch you."

What I want? She is already doing what I want. What more is there? "I don't understand."

"Taking the role of Prime," she clarifies, her tongue tracing a circle over my pulse. "Visualize it and hold onto it."

Ah, I understand now. This is a manifestation exercise. Certainly unlike any I have done before, but the basic concept is something I am quite familiar with. "Very well," I tell her, gripping her forearm as she begins to pump in and out of my core.

Closing my eyes, I picture the moment I announce that I am the main source of power in the coven, and I shall be taking Tibik's place immediately. I see his face, twisted and pinched in anger, as the rest of the coven gasps at my words.

"How does it feel, tiny witch?" Alu asks as she kisses along my collarbone. "You are the true leader of your coven. You are Prime."

My heartbeat quickens as my visualization turns into a series of images that flash through my mind. Images of Tibik admitting that my power is stronger than his and stepping down, of the coven coming together for the Prime inaugural ceremony, of us seated in a circle in the spell room and strengthening our craft together as one.

I feel my k'billita throb as her fingers brush against them, stroking them as my juices soak her hand.

"That is it," Alu says encouragingly. "The coven is yours now, Jo, and you have the freedom to guide them however you please."

Goddess, it is something I have not even allowed myself to dream about. It did not seem possible. But this vision fills me with unparalleled joy and hope. It feels like it is a reality within my grasp, but I must be bold enough to reach for it.

"Yes," Alu hisses as she uses her other hand to squeeze my swollen, aching nipples. "You are Prime now."

That is all it takes to send me careening over the edge as pure, consuming ecstasy blasts through my body. At one point, I open one eye and notice an orb in a bright white color radiating from my cunt as my hips jerk erratically against Alu's hand. I did not know I was capable of producing such power from a sexual encounter. I have yet to explore this aspect of my magic and the results such experimentation would yield.

"Wow," Alu says with a smug grin as she removes her fingers and sucks them clean. "That was the most spectacular thing I have ever seen."

"Me?" I ask, suddenly shy under her proud gaze.

"Yes, you," she says, wrapping her arm around me and shoving her nose into my mane. "The sheer power that lives inside your body, Jo. Magic is inside your very bones."

"I am not certain," I reply, downplaying her compliments. That is not exactly the biological makeup of a Hexrin, but I cannot deny my power is robust. I had no idea that producing an orb upon reaching release was possible until now. And it is all because of Alu. "Thank you," I tell her, pressing a kiss to her palm.

"For what?" she asks, aghast. "For making you come?"

"More than just that," I correct her. "But yes, for everything."

I turn to face her and tuck my head against her chest, right above her beating heart.

She runs her fingers through my mane. "The pleasure was all mine."

* * *

"I shall come with you!" Alu shouts, excitement brightening her expression as she shoves her feet into her silver ankle-high boots.

"No, no," I reply, trying to conceal the panic in my voice as I fasten the rope belt at my waist. "It is merely a meditation exercise that I must do when the sun is at its highest point in the sky. You will not find it interesting to watch." I cannot have her follow me to the edge of the dirt path and into the jungle. I must check the status of the dark energy cluster on my own.

She huffs a breath and crosses her arms over her chest. "That is simply not true. I could watch you clean the dishes, and I would find it interesting."

Three steps are all that separates us, and I close that distance to give her a long, smacking kiss. "I shall return soon." Then I race outside before she can shower me with more compliments.

Halfway down the dirt path, I find two long sticks that I break into several smaller pieces. Then I pull a thin, flexible wire from my pocket that I found in Alu's washroom and secure the six smaller sticks together into a hexagon.

Pressing the shape over my heart, I close my eyes and chant quietly,

Fra luyhivna u cinnqu srem il sa yon dyvha.

May this sacred talisman bring peace to this land.

Bathi yv ewq tennoh iz num purmik sa gen.

Keep my focus unwavering and my power strong.

Burgh oplya vr kai dineivah.

Protect my soul from the evil that persists.

I take a deep breath once I finish my chant and continue down the path. I have not even reached the end when every hair on my body stands at frightened attention, and the air becomes thick. It is as if I am stuck inside an invisible fog.

The cluster has moved.

I do not feel any overwhelming pain or discomfort, which means the talisman is working, but I am finding it difficult to breathe. Also, the fact that the energy cluster has shifted closer to Alu's home is deeply concerning. I do not know what will happen when it envelops her cottage entirely, or what will happen to Alu and Mek if they are still inside when it does.

Steeling my spine, I lift my palms in front of my chest, facing each other, and close my eyes. Separating part of the cluster to learn more about it did not work. But perhaps I can cut a hole through it from the inside in an effort to drain some of the energy. I focus my mind on the image of a sword made of gleaming steel and impressively long with a point so sharp, it could slice through several layers of solid ground and expose the molten core of Oluura to the elements. An orb in a rich shade of blue appears between my hands, and I hold it there, giving it time to grow and fortify.

Taking a step deeper into the cluster, I turn to face the outer edge that I just entered through, and flip my palms outward, shooting the orb into the side of it. The orb makes contact, and the blue circle expands as if it hit a solid wall. It stays that way for several heartbeats, making me wonder if it did anything to damage the cluster at all.

Sighing heavily, I repeat the exercise as another blue orb forms between my palms, but before I can shoot it toward the barrier, a crackling sound fills my ears and the original orb comes barreling toward me, twice as strong as when it left my hands. It hits me in the stomach, knocking the air from my lungs as I am thrown through the air, and land hard on my back halfway up the dirt path.

Gasping for breath, I turn onto my side as the dark energy cluster becomes visible. It drifts toward me like a grayish black storm cloud and spans the width of the entire jungle.

It becomes clear that there is no way to defeat this energy on my own. And I cannot protect Alu from it if it continues to move.

We must leave.

Today.

I race back to the cottage and burst through the front door.

"What is wrong?" Alu asks, leaping to her feet at the sight of me.

I told her I was going to meditate, but instead I am frantic, my clothes are dirt-stained, and my chest is heaving. "I-I think we should return to the clan," I blurt out.

Alu tilts her head to the side but says nothing.

"I am ready to face the coven. To face Tibik."

A smile tugs at the corners of her lips. "Truly?" she asks, coming toward me with arms outstretched.

I nod, relieved that she does not question my motives. "Yes, after my...my meditation, I feel ready to claim my role as Prime. I have hidden my power for far too long."

She wraps me in a tight hug, rubbing a hand down my back. "I am so proud of you," she whispers. When she pulls back to look at me, I see something new in her gaze. It is not merely admiration, as that I would recognize. It is not lust either, because I have seen that many times. It is both of those things, layered with something else. Though I suppose there is no time to analyze. We must leave before the cluster moves closer.

"Yes, well, it shall be a long flight back, so we should pack the necessities and begin our journey."

Alu throws a few clothing items into a small bag and stands waiting by the door. "Ready!"

I look at her, then the bag. "That is all you wish to bring? What about Mek?"

"He can remain here," she says. "I do not take him with me when I fly."

"Oh," I reply, my stomach sinking like a stone at the thought of Mek all alone here when the cluster surrounds the house. I still do not know the source of the energy, or what it seeks, but I know I cannot let it reach Mek. Alu would be devastated if anything were to happen to him. "I can carry him. He can sit on my shoulder inside your claw."

She gives me a strange look, so I quickly add, "You do not know how long you will be gone. I might want you to stay…a while."

Her gray eyes flash with longing. She *wants* this. She wants to be with me at the village.

Tibik will not be pleased by Alu's presence at the coven house, or Mek's, but I no longer care what Tibik has to say about anything.

Alu whistles and Mek comes flying out of his room, letting out a hysterical squawk as he lands on my shoulder. "Oof," I grunt when his claws sink into my skin.

"Shall we?" Alu asks, opening the front door for me.

"We shall."

CHAPTER 11

ALU

We arrive just after dusk, the tall blades of grass in the open field just outside the village tickling my large claws. Jo stretches her limbs once I release her, and Mek does the same in his own way. He leaps into the air and flies in a tight circle above our heads before settling onto Jo's shoulder.

I shift into my flightless form and feel the sudden urge to straighten my clothes. I am about to meet Jo's coven. Perhaps I should have changed into a clean shirt before we left.

"What is it?" Jo asks when she sees me fiddling with the bottom hem of my top.

"I…I just wish to make a good impression," I say with a sigh.

Jo laughs as she scrunches her nose. "You have met the clan before."

"I know," I reply, struggling to find the right words to explain what I am feeling. Eventually, I give up. "Mind me not. It is nothing."

Mek jumps from Jo's shoulder to mine as we enter the forest surrounding the village. The sound of distant laughter meets my ears, and I smile at the thought of Jo returning after such an awful event to finally claim her rightful place as Prime Hexrin. It takes a great amount of courage to do such a thing, even though Nalba's injury was not her fault.

I do not think anyone blames Jo for Nalba's memory loss, either, but my tiny witch has a soft heart, and—

Wait.

When did I start thinking of her as *my* tiny witch? No, Jo is just *a* tiny witch that I am currently having magnificent, life-giving sex with, and that is all there is to it. She is certainly not mine. She cannot be. I have no mate. My handlers said as much.

I also do not wish for Jo to be put in a position where she must choose between me and her coven because I know she will not choose me.

"Jo!" a voice calls the moment we step onto the main path that runs through the center of the village. It is Ava, the healer with the puffy black hair and the sparkling smile. "Alu, hi!" she adds gleefully when she sees me. She gives Jo a hug and reaches her arms out toward me to do the same, but Mek caws loudly, causing Ava to back away and offer a small wave instead.

Soon we are surrounded by members of the clan, buzzing with excitement at Jo's return, and cautiously curious by my presence at her side. I overhear a few whispers from the golden beings with the same maroon hair that Jo has—members of the coven—though I cannot make out the words they spoke. I assume it is about me, though, by the strange looks I am receiving.

Kate and Niro approach the edge of the crowd, and when Kate sees my horns, she pushes her way through. I hear "Pregnant lady coming through" as she places a hand on her growing belly, and everyone instantly takes a step back to give her room.

"You're back!" she cheers when she reaches us. She notices the bird on my shoulder and tries to mask a slight grimace. "Oh, hey, Mek."

"You have brought the bird here," Nirossanai says haughtily. "Why?"

Bracing myself for another lecture on how I should send Mek back into the jungle, I sigh. But before he can say another word, Jo reaches up to stroke Mek's beak, and says, "Mek is family. We chose not to leave him behind."

My brother looks taken aback by Jo's response, or perhaps it is because she responded at all. Either way, I am pleased when he does not speak another word.

The clan leads us directly to the food hall, and we take our seats between Kate and Niro and Chloe and Varrek at the table in the center. Plates stacked high with junasii bread, some kind of root mash, and berries are put in front of us. The coven does not join us at the table, and I do not see them after we begin eating.

"Here," a gruff voice says from behind me, just as two mugs filled with frothy orange liquid are placed in front of us, the liquid sloshing over the sides. "Ale."

It was the scarred male who led the battle against Bzzsil Chi, I notice as he stomps off. "Thank you!" I call out, but I do not think he hears me.

The new human females are seated at the very end of the table— there are five of them—and they are shooting assessing glances our way.

The table grows quiet as we focus on our meals, with occasional friendly chatter and questions about Jo's stay at Kate and Niro's caves. It does not seem as if anyone here knows that Jo has been staying with me for the last several days. I suppose that is fine, as I am not sure how I would explain the reason for it.

"I lied and said my bird friend was possessed so that I could shove my tongue inside Jo's delectable cunt" does not seem like the kind of statement the clan would be eager to hear. Not during mealtime, anyway.

Kate's gaze returns to us repeatedly, a secret smile playing on her lips as she watches each interaction I have with Jo. She does not prod, however, which I appreciate.

Once we finish our meals, I follow Jo to the coven house and up to her room. "Oh," she says, disappointment deepening the creases in her brow as she looks around the space we are going to share. There is a bed, but it has been pushed against the far wall, and several items are scattered atop the blankets and all over the floor. "I guess they have been using my room for spell practice."

Mek leaps off my shoulder and flies in a loop around the room before settling into the deepest part of one of Jo's many pillows while she and I gather the items from the bed and floor and place them in the corner of the room.

"I see you have returned."

Jo gasps at the sound of the male's voice as she whirls around to face him.

Ah, Tibik.

He leans against the door frame with his arms crossed, the crinkles around his mouth and eyes growing tighter. I can tell he means to intimidate with his posture and tone, but it does not work. A single flick of my finger against his forehead would send him flying through the walls and into the bushes outside.

"She has," I reply, straightening my spine and lifting my chin defiantly. "And she is not going anywhere."

Tibik purses his lips as his squinty gaze moves over me. "Why is *she* here?" he asks Jo without looking away from me. This male tries to intimidate me, but he fails again.

"I am with her," I reply, silently daring him to question us further.

He chooses not to and eventually walks away while grumbling something under his breath.

Jo closes the door behind him with a huff. "I need to speak with him tomorrow, and I am not looking forward to it."

"Speak with him about what? The role of Prime?" I ask.

"Shh!" she scolds, putting a finger to her lips. "I do not want him to discover my plans before I can put them in motion."

"That is fair," I tell her as I undress and climb beneath the thick furs piled high on her bed.

Jo does the same, and her arms instinctively wrap around me, pulling me against her body. Being in this strange, crowded house makes me hesitant to follow my desires. If we were at my cottage, I would flip Jo onto her back and shove my face between her thighs, but being here in her home seems to weigh on her brilliant mind. She deserves to feel comfort right now, and while I cannot change the mood throughout the house, I can provide contentment with my embrace. And I do not mind doing so. Not in the slightest.

I lie on my side so I can look at her, running my fingers along her forehead, through her spiky dark-red hair, and along her sharp, perfect cheekbones as her eyes get heavier. "Sleep well, tiny witch," I whisper the moment her eyelids fall closed.

Mek shakes out his feathers before he turns and settles into a different position on the pillow directly above Jo's head, and I worry the movement will wake her, but thankfully, it does not, and I follow both of them into a deep sleep shortly thereafter.

* * *

The next day passes quickly and without incident. Kate and Niro ask us to join them for a leisurely walk to the nearby falls. Mek flies alongside us part of the way, but at some point, he disappears, and I assume he is on the hunt for berries. Kate grumbles at one point about us walking too fast, and that she "can only waddle as quickly as the growing draxilio inside her gut will allow," but once we slow our pace, her cheerful demeanor returns.

At some point, Niro leaps into the air to grab a colorful leaf from a high branch. He hands it to Kate and her eyes swirl with desire. I do the same, jumping up to pull a prettier leaf from an even higher branch, and I cannot resist the smug smile that tugs at my lips knowing I can jump higher than him.

Upon returning from our walk, Nalba races up to us and wraps Jo in a tight hug. It is clear Jo was not expecting this by the utter confusion swirling in her eyes.

"Nalba," Jo says when Nalba finally releases her. "I am so pleased to see you in such great health."

"Jo, you saved me," Nalba says, taking both of Jo's hands in hers.

Jo nods. "Ah, I have heard you are now mated to Waldric. Many blessings and good tidings to you both."

"No, Jo," Nalba says. "Well, yes, I am with Waldric, and he is the perfect male for me. But that is not what I meant. This," she adds, reaching for the necklace she is wearing. "This saved me. I did not believe in magic before, but you have left me to question whether it is real."

"Well, it is real," Jo replies with a teasing grin. "I can assure you of that."

"Do you wish to have it back?" Nalba asks, turning the necklace around and fiddling with the clasp.

"No," Jo says instantly, holding up her hands. "That is a necklace I made for you. The protection spell I put on it only applies to you. Please, keep it."

Nalba hugs Jo again and says something about how she must return to her shop before scurrying down the path. I notice Jo's gaze lingering on Nalba's retreating form. A deep exhale releases the tension in Jo's shoulders, and it looks as if she is finally at peace with what happened during the battle against Bzzsil Chi.

Shortly after, I am introduced to the tr'gory pup called Stanley, whose tongue hangs from the side of his mouth as he jumps and shoves his paws into my stomach. It does not knock me down, but it does cause me to stagger a few steps before regaining my balance. His human mother, Eleanor, tells me he is growing rapidly.

"Sorry about the jumping," she says, her cheeks pink with embarrassment. "We're working on it."

"*She* is working on it," her mate, Bruvix, the one who makes ale, adds as he gestures toward Eleanor with a soft smile. "Stahn-lee is not working on anything and is a terrible listener."

"No, he's not," Eleanor protests as she scratches Stanley's head between his tall white horns. "He's a good boy. Aren't you, Stanley?"

Stanley does not answer her question. He merely leans his large body against her leg and tilts his head back against Eleanor's knee when her hand leaves his head—a silent plea for her to continue her scratching.

I am quite charmed by the members of the clan I have spent time with today. Jo seems to be in a better mood as well, which settles my insides.

A loud, angry squawk pulls our attention to the right, and I take off in a sprint toward it. I hear Jo's light footsteps behind me, and we reach the coven house within moments to find Tibik just outside the front door, waving a long dagger at Mek, who is flapping his wings and remains just out of Tibik's reach.

"What is the meaning of this?" I shout.

Tibik drops the dagger to the ground, his cheeks puffing out with each labored breath, and points an accusatory finger in my direction. "Your filthy bird relieved himself all over my cloak." Then his eyes land on Jo. "He does not belong in this house. We cannot focus on our craft with this beast constantly disrupting us."

"Mek," I say, tapping the tips of my claws together to make the clacking noise that signals him to come. He obeys my command and lands softly on my shoulder.

The members of the coven who have gathered outside to witness Tibik's dramatic outburst eventually follow the cranky Hexrin inside, leaving Jo and me alone. Her expression is pained, and her body is as still as a statue.

I am surprised by this. She seemed so ready to put Tibik in his place. Is that not why we flew here so hastily, so she could have the confrontation she has been dreading and finally get it over with?

I stride over to her and place my hand on her shoulder. "Do not worry. Mek is just used to his routines at the cottage. It will take some time for him to adapt, but he will."

Jo's gaze remains on the front door of the coven house as if she is waiting for Tibik to storm back out and continue yelling at her. At us.

I would never let someone speak to one I cared about the way Jo just let Tibik speak to me. I know she has been timid and fearful far longer than she has been a powerful, confident witch, but still, I was not expecting to encounter such blatant rudeness.

"Come," I tell her, pulling her into my side as I drape my arm over her shoulders. "All will be well."

We go inside and climb the steps to her bedroom, avoiding the eyes of everyone we pass. Why is the coven not more excited about Jo's return? I do not understand their silence, given how miserable it must have been with just Tibik leading them.

Jo kicks off her boots and crawls into bed. She does not get under the blankets. She just pulls a pillow against her chest and curls into a tight ball. Mek flies across the room and settles himself into his spot on the pillow above her.

I hate seeing her this dejected. It makes me want to shift into my draxilio and fly us back to my cottage where we can be alone and content once again.

It also makes me want to unleash a ball of fire onto Tibik's face and melt the permanently sour expression right off his skull.

Yes! my draxilio purrs. *We should do that! Defend our mate!*

Whoa, she is not our mate, I send back.

I do not know exactly what Jo is to me at this point. She is more than just a female I have successfully seduced. I cannot seem to get enough of her in that regard. There is not a moment that passes when I do not want to feel her lips against mine.

While this is a new experience for me, and the feelings I have for Jo are also new, I am not convinced it means she is my mate.

But I still wish to care for her in any way that she will allow. "What can I do?" I ask as I rub her back.

She turns to face me, her eyes filled with unshed tears, and my draxilio growls low in my chest. She, too, has grown quite attached to this tiny witch. "Water?" Jo asks.

I press a kiss to her hair before I go downstairs to fetch her some water. Just as I finish filling a glass jug with water from the spigot, Tibik enters the room and sighs heavily when he sees me. I choose to ignore him entirely as I go to climb the stairs.

"You do not belong here," he says, halting my steps. "You and your obnoxious bird."

I take a long sip of water, keeping my gaze locked on his as the liquid slides down my throat before I say, "Jo wants me here. I am not leaving her side unless she requests that I do." Then I turn on my heel and head back upstairs.

I am halfway up the staircase when I hear Tibik chuckle snidely and say, "Hexrins are prohibited from taking a mate. Even if that were not the case, she would never choose someone like you."

Someone like me.

What does that mean? Because I am a draxilio?

Or is he referring to my genetic modifications?

Does he think just because I was modified to lack fear that I am not smart or composed enough to be mated to a Hexrin? That I am not worthy of standing at Jo's side?

What if I continue to become more attached to her? Will that put her in a position where she has to choose between me and her coven? I know she will choose her coven, and I would not blame her for it. Her witchcraft is in her blood.

Then my mind drifts to the day I cut my arm after missing the rope over the pool. Jo was quite angry with me. Just as she was when I went outside to feed the feathered reptilian creature on the balcony.

Perhaps…Tibik is right.

Perhaps Mek and I are too wild to live among the clan with their structured mealtimes and daily chores. Perhaps the jungle is the only place we truly belong.

CHAPTER 12

JO

It has only been two days since Alu and I returned from her cottage, and the tension in the coven house is as thick as the dark energy cluster in the jungle. I do not know how to resume my coven duties while leaving enough time to spend with Alu.

She remains close by all the time, which I appreciate because she is trying to protect me from Tibik's cutting remarks, but it is a small house, and Alu is a large presence. It does not help that Mek has been an absolute menace.

The only time Mek is not wreaking havoc is when he is asleep on the pillow above my head. The rest of the time, he is pooping on people's clothes, squawking in their ears, or using his claws to rip apart their bedding for a new nest.

Put Mek and Alu together in a house with four other Hexrins and Tibik, and it is a constant state of chaos.

I am also a bit stressed because I need to have a conversation with Tibik about what happened during the battle with Bzzsil Chi, but I have not summoned the courage to broach the subject. When he is not criticizing me under his breath in front of the rest of the coven, he is complaining loudly about Alu or Mek, or both.

It has been easier to avoid the subject altogether. Because I know the moment I reopen this wound, it will not just be the battle we argue about, but every other moment of unpleasantness that has passed between us over the last two centuries.

That is what happens when Tibik's choices are questioned. He gets defensive and lashes out with a list of mistakes the person questioning him has made, and the original point of the discussion gets lost.

Alu is also growing frustrated by my stalling. She has not said as much to me, but I can tell in the way her jaw clenches every time Tibik speaks, and then in the silence that follows when I do not stand up to him.

Her disappointment is like a dagger plunged deep into my side, and with each additional opportunity to confront Tibik that I am too afraid to take, the knife twists deeper.

I am not a fire-breathing draxilio who was altered to lack fear, however. I am just a short, timid Hexrin who has been pretending to be weaker than I am for the last two hundred years. After playing the part for so long, I have started to believe it. A handful of days in the jungle pretending to be worthy of the role of Prime cannot erase the time I have spent cowering in the corner.

Right now, what I must focus on is bringing the coven together. Well, everyone but Tibik. We have spent far too much time apart, and the younger Hexrins need my guidance. They are certainly not getting it from our leader.

"Let us begin. Who would like to lead this morning's invocation to the goddess?" I ask, looking around the circle. Our three other Hexrins, Rulya, Divahni, and Qayeko, are all quite timid, and sit silently as they drop their gazes to the ground. We are seated in the small clearing next to the house since the rituals we have attempted inside the house have proved…difficult. Eventually, Rulya, our youngest Hexrin at one hundred three, raises her hand.

"Wonderful, Rulya," I cheer. "Today we are calling upon the goddess to keep our soil free of frost during the cold season so that our crops may continue to thrive."

We join hands, inhale deeply, and close our eyes.

Rulya clears her throat and begins the invocation "Goddess above, giver of light and life alike, we call upo–"

"Mek! Get back here!" Alu shouts as she chases Mek out the front door and around the outside of the house.

Our circle is broken by the disruption, and I sigh in frustration as I get to my feet. "What has he done now?" I ask.

"He tore the hood…" Alu grunts as she leaps into the air, trying to grab hold of Mek's tail feathers, "off your cloak."

"My cloak?" I repeat, my voice rising to a squeaky, distressed pitch. Now I will have to ask Zohma to repair it, and the sewing circle is always so busy with clothing repairs that they may not get around to it until we are nearing the end of the cold season. By then, I will not need a hood at all.

"Gahh," she groans when Mek flies away, heading deeper into the forest. She places her hands on her hips and turns toward us, her eyes lighting up at the sight of our circle. "Are you meditating?" she asks as she approaches the blanket spread out beneath us. "I am in dire need of some meditation."

A sharp crunch beneath Alu's foot has us all whipping our heads around. When she lifts her boot, Rulya sucks in a breath as she gathers the broken, tattered remains of the wreath she made as an offering to the goddess, wrapped in herbs and flowers that are now destroyed. She clutches it to her chest as her cheeks darken, and I know she is on the verge of tears.

"Many apologies," Alu says with a pained expression as she softly pats Rulya's shoulder. "I did not see it."

"This seems like a good time for a break," I tell the group, trying to distract Rulya enough to keep her from crying. I can tell Alu already feels terrible, and I do not wish to make the situation worse for anyone. "Let us reconvene our circle after middle meal, yes?"

The Hexrins rise to their feet and head in the direction of the food hall as I gather the supplies from our circle to take them inside.

"Something ails you," Alu says, lifting the blanket from the ground and shaking it out. "Tell me what it is."

"No, no," I say, trying to reassure her, "all is well. I am just distracted, I suppose." I do not tell her she is the distraction because I do not wish to hurt her feelings, but I do not know what to do. If there was another house she could stay in, I would suggest she do so, but with the recent arrival of the five human females, every free bed in the village is occupied.

If we were to continue strengthening the connection between us, how would it even work? I cannot ask her to abandon her cottage in the jungle when I cannot take a mate. Though, if the dark energy cluster remains on her property, she really should abandon it.

I also do not know how she truly feels about me. She brought me to her cottage to seduce me, which she has. How much longer will she remain interested in spending time with me? If she wants nothing more than a pleasure mate, that would be fine with me. I just wish I knew for certain.

Of course, I could always come out and ask the question. But asking Alu a question like that is almost as terrifying as pondering what her answer might be. She does not soften her delivery, no matter the situation. What if I ask her how she feels about me, and her answer is that she feels nothing beyond the joy of physical release?

After what we have shared, the things she has done to my body, the emotions she has awoken inside me, I am not certain I could handle hearing such a statement from her lips without instantly crumbling.

We return the invocation supplies to the storage box just inside the front door, and Alu pulls me into her arms. "You need a different kind of distraction, I think," she says, pressing a gentle kiss to each of my knuckles.

"Is that so?" I ask, a familiar flutter of excitement filling my belly as she pulls me up the stairs. At last, we have time to ourselves. I have missed the feel of her bare skin against mine.

By the time we get inside my room, I am rubbing myself against her shamelessly as her hands squeeze and massage my behind. "You smell so good today," she purrs as she runs her nose along the length of my throat.

"Better than yesterday?" I ask, pretending to be offended, but mostly curious as to how I would smell different today compared to yesterday.

She chuckles as she lifts the hem of my tunic and pulls it over my head. "You smell good every day." Her lips surround my nipple the moment a knock sounds at my bedroom door.

A menacing growl rips from Alu's throat.

"Yes?" I shout, knowing it must be Tibik. The others are at the food hall, and I am not expecting them to return for a while.

"I must speak with you," he says in an agitated tone.

I let out a growl of my own as I put my tunic back on and step out into the hallway. "What is it?" I ask.

"I have just come from the food hall," he says, his chin lifted defiantly. Though I am not sure why, because he still has not given a reason for interrupting me and Alu.

"And? What happened at the food hall?"

"Rulya was quite saddened by the destruction of her wreath," he whispers, tilting his head in Alu's direction.

Ah, that is what this is about. He is using this as another reason to protest Alu's presence in our home. "Alu apologized immediately. She did not mean to break it."

He looks at my closed bedroom door, then back at me before he takes my arm and pulls me down the hall into his bedroom. "She cannot remain here," he says at a normal volume now that Alu cannot hear us. "Why do you continue with this silly charade?"

"I do not understand what you mean."

"Yes, you do," he says as he crosses his arms over his chest. "You cannot take a mate, you know this. So while you may be having fun with her now, eventually, you will have to end it."

I hate that I cannot dismiss his words as blatant lies. There is truth in them.

"Do you wish to hurt her?" he asks.

The answer comes easily. "No. I never want to cause her pain."

"Then you need to end it now."

He says nothing more. He just opens the door to his room and gestures for me to leave. I am left wondering how I am supposed to let Alu go when everything inside me screams to remain at her side until my very last breath.

CHAPTER 13

ALU

When Jo returns to her room, her mood has changed dramatically. It is clearly something Tibik said, but I cannot get her to share it with me. She is distant and cold, and nothing like the strong, tiny witch I got to know in the jungle.

Being here changes her. She is still the object of my desires, but this version of Jo is a mere shell of who she could be, of who I know she is deep within.

I shake my head as I watch her fold and unfold that same tunic three times. "I do not understand why you let him manipulate your thoughts."

"He does no such thing," she replies, sounding unconvinced by her own words.

"Yes, he does."

When she remains silent, my draxilio fills my head with ideas on how to handle this Tibik.

Melt his lips together! Then he can never utter another word!

What a gratifying image. Yes, that sounds like a brilliant plan. "I shall handle this," I tell Jo, getting off the bed and striding toward the door. Before I reach it, Jo grabs me by the wrist.

"No. Alu, please do not get involved. I can handle it on my own."

"Can you?" I ask, searching her face for the dominant Hexrin I know is in there.

She lets go of my arm, and I notice her posture stiffen. "Yes, I can. I just need some space to do this on my own. I do not need you to fight my battles for me."

"But I want to fight your battles for you," I tell her. "So that you do not have to fight at all." Why is it so hard for her to understand this? She is strong enough to do this herself, but since I am here by her side, she does not need to. It would be an honor to destroy Tibik for her. I spent several soliqs as one of the king's assassins on Sufoi. Fighting another person's battles is something I am extremely proficient in.

"Well, I do not want you to!" she shouts, throwing the tunic she keeps folding to the floor.

"Right," I say quietly as I stare at the tunic. "You wish for space."

She nods as she plops down on the edge of the bed.

"Very well," I reply, shoving my feet into my boots. "Then I shall give you space." I throw the bedroom door open and storm down the stairs. I do not stop until I reach the main path, and by then, my entire body is trembling with rage.

"Alussanai," Niro says as he spots me. "Where are you off to?" By the time he reaches me, he must see the fury I am struggling to contain. His expression softens and he nods knowingly. "Come. Fly with me."

I follow my brother on foot through the forest and into the large clearing. We launch into the sky, and he is the first to turn his giant draxilio head upward and unleash a steady stream of fire into the clouds.

I hear him chuckle inside my head through the mental link we share when we are in this form at the same time. *Let it out,* he sends. *Unleash your pain through your flame.*

It is a coping mechanism our handlers taught us not long after we first learned to shift. Before we had control of our power, we were only allowed to breathe fire into the sky, where it would not cause anyone harm.

There is nothing I want more than to cause harm, but only to one person: Tibik. But since Jo does not want me to do so, I will resist the urge. Instead, I will relieve this frustration by chasing my brother through the air, sending balls of fire dangerously (but amusingly) close to his tail.

CHAPTER 14

JO

Rulya concludes the invocation to the goddess, offering a small bouquet of flowers she picked near the falls after middle meal earlier. It is not as nice as the wreath she made, but it is enough that the goddess will appreciate her efforts. Together, the four of us close the circle and place our offerings at the base of the small outdoor altar we set up next to the house.

The sound of shouting and clapping draws me toward the main path, and I continue to follow the sound until I reach the edge of the crowd gathered at the entrance to the training grounds. Flames fill the sky and the crowd oohs and ahhs as they back away from the wide opening to the space, giving me a clear view of what is happening.

It appears to be a competition of some kind between Alu and Nee-roh, who are both in their draxilio forms.

Kayt's bright red mane catches my eye, and I race to her side. "What is this?" I ask.

"Ugh," she says, rolling her eyes. "Sibling rivalry, apparently, because an innocent flight between Niro and Alu has led to a weird competition to see who can do the most consecutive flips in the air while still in dragon form."

Alu is currently shaking her draxilio head as she stretches her wings. It must be her turn next. Nee-roh's draxilio is bigger and wider than hers, which makes me think she would be better at this.

"Who is winning?" I ask Kayt.

"So far, it's Niro in the lead with six consecutive flips. But Alu has five, so it's close."

"What are they competing for?"

Kayt shrugs. "Pride, I guess."

The moment Alu launches into the air, my heart leaps into my throat. I do not breathe or think as I watch her impressively large form curl into a tight ball in midair. The light bounces off her cerulean scales, making her look as if her entire body is sparkling in the sun. The crowd lets out an excited cheer after Alu's first flip, then again after her second.

Her body lowers in the sky after the third flip, and she needs to unfurl herself quickly in order to flap her wings and regain the height she lost.

Flips four and five are smooth, but she sinks again after the sixth. She is now tied with Nee-roh, and I expect her to flap her wings in order to get the height she needs to work in a few more flips, but she does not.

Instead, gravity pulls her draxilio closer to the ground as she ducks her large head into her chest and attempts a seventh flip. But her body tilts slightly to the right, and the clan lets out a collective gasp as she comes close to crashing into the mass of bodies. Then everyone is screaming and running away from the training grounds as Alu strug-gles to flap her wings hard enough to remain in the air.

She avoids the crowd, but in an effort to right her path, she twists inward and her long, spiked tail collides with the stone beam holding up the open entrance to the food hall. The roof collapses on the right side, crashing into the cooking station and destroying most of the fire pits Waldric and Krahn use to cook our meals.

A hush falls over the crowd as we stand there and take in the destruction. It took the clan three moon cycles to build the food hall. All of us helped. And now, it is so badly damaged that I am not certain if it can be salvaged at all.

Alu shifts into her flightless form and staggers to her feet, shaking her head as if trying to shake the dizziness from her skull. She looks at the mess and shoots a sheepish grin my way. "Many apologies. I lost control and did not see where I was going."

"Many apologies," I mutter through gritted teeth.

"What?" she asks, leaning closer and waiting for me to elaborate.

Suddenly, the stress of the last several days hits me from every direction. I am tired of Tibik's judgmental gaze every time he sees me. I am tired of apologizing for Mek's awful behavior. I am tired of Alu making reckless choices and leaving a mess in her wake. Mostly, I am just tired. "Many apologies?" I repeat, this time in a shout. "Look at what you have done to our food hall!"

Alu jerks back as if struck. "It was not intentional, Jobaki. I shall help repair it."

That is not enough. "What will the clan do for food until it is repaired? How will Waldric and Krahn feed us without the fire pits? We are in the cold season, Alu. We cannot rely on our crops to keep us fed. If the frost comes, we will need to survive on the preserved jerky and stale bread that we keep for the hunters. If we run out of that, we could starve!"

She takes a step closer and reaches for me, but I hold up a hand, stopping her where she stands. Her shoulders slump forward as she lowers her gaze to the ground. "I would not let you or your people starve, Jo. You must know that."

Her visible pain threatens to send me to my knees. I do not wish to hurt her, but I cannot allow this recklessness to continue. Not here in the village. Not in the coven house where I am responsible for the success of the younger Hexrins. If I hope to ever summon the courage to confront Tibik and take the role of Prime, I must be able to make tough decisions like this. It is for the good of the coven, and I am a Hexrin before all else.

"I cannot do this anymore," I say, my voice barely a whisper as the words leave my mouth. I regret them instantly, but I do not take them back. As much as it will hurt me to let Alu go, I must. It is what is best for all of us.

"Do what?" she asks, confused as she searches my face. Realization hits just a moment later, and tears sting my eyes as she nods, defeated. "Very well."

She starts to walk away, but then freezes in place, and whips around with fury tightening her features. "Enjoy another two centuries of misery, Jobaki."

"I am not miserable. I am…happy," I bark out. It is not true. I am the opposite of happy, but I am not prepared to admit that publicly.

"No, you are not," she shouts. "And you never will be until you find a way to face what frightens you."

"Well," I shout back, "you will need to realize that fear or no fear, you cannot make reckless decisions if you hope to share your life with another. It is selfish."

She swipes angrily at her cheeks, trying to hide her tears. "Then this goodbye could not come at a better time." Kayt and Nee-roh approach slowly and wrap their arms around Alu as they guide her away from me, toward the clearing outside the forest.

Then I remember the dark energy cluster near her cottage, and my palms begin to sweat at the idea of her returning home unprotected.

Kayt shoots me an empathetic glance over her shoulder, and it tells me she is not angry at me for what just happened, which is a relief, but it does not make me feel any less devastated or afraid for Alu's safety. I close my eyes to focus on the open portal inside Kayt's mind. It is often wide open for anyone to communicate with her as her power has yet to reach the point where she can close it.

I find her power receptive, as I had hoped, and plant a thought in her mind that I hope she assumes came to her naturally. *Take Alu to the caves. She should not be alone.* And I silently pray Kayt will do just that.

Members of the clan slowly gather around the food hall and begin clearing away the debris. I sense movement to my right and hold back a sound of disgust when I realize it is Tibik. His lips are curved up in a smile that he is not even trying to hide from me. "That was the right decision," he says, placing a hand on my arm.

I jerk out of his grasp and curl my lips back in a snarl when I turn to face him. "Lay a hand on me again and I will slice your throat while you sleep."

His eyes widen in horror, and it fills me with intense, consuming euphoria. If I do not get to spend my life with Alu, then I *will* be Prime Hexrin of this coven, and Tibik needs to watch his back.

CHAPTER 15

ALU

I cannot sleep. Food tastes like bitter sludge in my mouth. Even Mek is more agitated than normal, but that could be due to the low light in Niro and Kate's caves. He has been flying in circles in the room I used to occupy when we first settled here after being banished from Sufoi. It is the same room I stay in whenever I visit Niro, but after living in the jungle for so long, this room no longer feels like mine. It is a spare room that just happens to have my old blankets in it.

Mek is perched on the iron bed frame at the foot of the bed, letting out an occasional shrill caw as he stares at me.

"What is it you want?" I ask impatiently. "We cannot go back to the jungle just yet, so you will need to get used to the caves. I am not ready to be alone out there."

Mek tilts his head as if to say, "So I suppose I am invisible then?"

"No," I quickly add. "It is not that your company is lacking, there is just…too many memories in that cottage. Memories I am not prepared to face yet."

He squawks in response, the sound laced with a whiny edge. He misses Jo. He is not alone in that.

"She does not want me anymore," I tell him, my voice cracking on the final word. My vision blurs with tears, and soon I am sobbing into the pillow clutched against my chest. I have cried several times since Kate and Niro brought me back to the caves yesterday, and I am surprised my tear ducts have not run dry.

"Knock, knock," Niro says as he raps his knuckles against the door.

I sniffle, trying to will my tears to stop falling. "You do not have to say it if you are doing it, brother."

He opens the door just a sliver to poke his head in. "Alussanai, are you well?"

"No!" I shout, throwing the pillow across the room. What a foolish question. Of course I am not well. My heart has just been cracked right down the center.

He sighs against the door frame, shoving his hands into the pockets of his dark gray pants. "Perhaps you should join me in the eating room."

I turn away from him and plop down onto my side. "I am not hungry."

The door creaks loudly as it is opened all the way. "But we are having tibbi," a deep, growly voice adds.

"Kulissanai!" I yell when I turn to find him standing next to Niro. Launching myself off the bed, I race to him and leap into his arms. He stands frozen at first, which is normal when I hug him. But I do not care that he refuses to hug me back because he is here. That is all that matters.

"Please join us before I am forced to swallow another mug of this slop," Kuli says as I release him, his bored tone echoing off the walls of the cave.

I run full speed down the hall. Sliding into the eating room, I find Kate sitting at the long table.

"Oh," I say, disappointment thick in my tone. "I was hoping Bexos-sanai would be here."

"Sorry, babe," Kate replies with an empathetic frown. "We sent him several comms and he never responded. He must be busy with the farm."

"That farm holds too much of his focus," Niro adds with a groan.

I take a seat next to Kuli and throw back a large glass of tibbi, my favorite beverage made from bokna fruit from the trees around my cottage. Kate refills it immediately.

"Now, tell us what has happened," Kuli says, resting his elbows on the table. "Who has caused you such pain and how do we go about destroying them?"

Kate and I yell "No!" at the same time.

"No one is going to touch Jo," I say through gritted teeth as I meet my brothers' gazes. "You shall not go near her. Is that understood?"

Niro holds up a hand. "I have no interest in harming Jo, but I cannot promise I will not go near her, as we spend much of our time with the clan."

The image of him and Kate having meals with Jo, or witnessing Jo practice her magic, fills me with crippling envy. They are so lucky to still have a place among the clan. Whereas I have nothing.

"Why are we gathering here if not to avenge Alussanai's pain?" Kuli asks, shaking his head in disappointment.

"We're here to offer support, just as you all did for me when I thought I had lost Kate for good," Niro says with a level of warmth in his tone that I am not used to. My heart squeezes when he shoots me a wink.

Mek caws loudly as he does a loop around the eating room, then leaves just as quickly to fly down the hall.

"Why is there a dirty, feathered critter flying around your caves, brother?" Kuli asks Niro.

I watch as measured restraint tightens his features. "It is, um, Alussanai's companion. She brought him with her from the jungle."

"Ick," Kuli mutters with a look of sheer disgust. "Birds are filthy creatures who should remain outdoors." Then he turns toward me. "Did you consider the mess this *thing* will cause in your home?"

"Well, I—" I begin, ready to explain that Mek has lived in my cottage with me since the day I finished building it, and that the mess he creates is confined to the room he occupies, but I do not get the chance to say any of that as Kuli interrupts.

"You truly did not think this decision through, Alussanai," he says with an incredulous chuckle. "Did you?"

We seem to have reached the part of the conversation where my brothers pick apart my lifestyle and my choices, and for once, I do not have the energy to try to convince them they are wrong. I am just…so very sick of being seen as a fool who cannot take care of herself. I have almost reached my third century of being alive. If I could not properly care for myself, I would be dead by now, would I not?

I say none of this to my brothers, however. I simply rise from my seat and walk out of the eating room.

"Where are you going?" Kuli shouts.

I pause just outside the door to the eating room and turn to face him with a shrug. "I am not interested in being the object of your ridicule. If this is how you plan to support me in my time of need, I would rather you left and returned home." I take a moment to revel in the look of shock on Kuli's and Niro's faces before I turn back toward my room.

Heavy footsteps follow me into the hall, and suddenly, both of them are standing in front of me, elbowing each other as their large bodies fill the narrow hallway. Kate arrives at my side with a gentle, caring smile on her face.

"Where is this coming from?" Niro asks.

Kuli says nothing, just crosses his arms over his wide chest and waits for me to speak.

There is no point in keeping these feelings to myself any longer. I did not even realize how deeply they were affecting me until recently. Until Jo. Before that, I let my brothers talk down to me, yell at me, criticize me for every decision I made simply because there was no one present who said, *No, Alussanai's mind is not like yours, but that does not mean there is something wrong with it.*

I believed them because they are my brothers, my family, and I assumed if they were frustrated with me, then they had a good reason to be. But I am starting to see that, after centuries of their mockery, perhaps they have been wrong about me.

"I do not enjoy feeling like I am your stupid, impulsive burden," I tell them. "You have always treated me as such, and it hurts."

Niro's mouth falls open. Creases form in Kuli's brow.

"I did not choose to exist this way, without fear, but you act as if it is something I can control," I explain, my spine straightening with each word. "You do not mock each other for your genetic modifications the same way you mock me."

Niro scrubs a hand down his face. Kuli absently scratches his chin.

I expect them to respond to my words, to say something, but they do not.

"Well?" Kate shouts, throwing her hands up. "Are you going to apologize to your sister for being complete assholes or what?"

I hear "I am sorry" and "Sincerest apologies, Alussanai" said at almost the same time.

"I can't believe you guys have treated her this way for almost three goddamn centuries!" Kate yells, taking my hand in hers. "You're lucky she even gave you the opportunity to apologize after such horrific behavior."

Niro steps forward and pulls me into a warm embrace. "I am so very sorry, sister," he says softly as he rubs a hand up and down my back. It is a level of affection I am not used to from him, and I find it odd, yet precisely the kind of comfort I need.

I return his embrace and lean my head against his chest, and the tears appear out of nowhere. "Thank you," I whisper back.

I feel more arms come around me as Kate and Kulissanai join the hug, and even though my face is soaked with tears, I cannot help but giggle at the sight of my ferocious, cold brothers bending to the demands of a small, pregnant human.

Kate may be new to the world of witchcraft, but it is clear her power is endless.

The hug ends and the four of us separate, and it is then that I look around for Mek. I have not heard his restless caw since he flew out of the eating room, and I begin to wonder where in the caves he has flown off to. When I turn to look down the hall, I notice the door to the launch cavern is ajar.

"Mek?" I call, striding toward the large, empty room. Kate and my brothers follow behind.

"What is wrong?" Kuli asks.

"I am looking for Mek. It is not like him to remain quiet for so long."

The moment I step into the launch cavern, my heart sinks into my stomach. "Why is the glass ceiling open like that?" I ask Niro.

His gaze turns accusatory when it lands on Kuli. "Did you not ensure that it was closed after you landed?"

Kuli jerks back with a defensive scowl. "I thought it was programmed to close automatically."

"Well, what is the concern here?" Niro asks. "He is a bird. Does he not fly freely most of the time?"

"He does," I admit. "But he is not familiar with this area. I just…I worry about him trying to find our cottage and getting lost."

Kate laces her fingers through mine and squeezes. "He'll be fine, Alu. I'm sure of it. When we were in the village, he was allowed to explore on his own and he always came back to you, right?"

"I suppose," I say with a heavy sigh.

She nods, hope swirling in her light green eyes. "Then we'll just leave the ceiling open for him, and I'm sure he'll be back soon."

Kate speaks the truth, and perhaps I should not be so worried about Mek's safety. I felt better having him close by, especially right now, because I cannot help but think that Jo left me, and now Mek has left too, and I wonder if I am meant to spend the rest of my life this way—alone.

CHAPTER 16

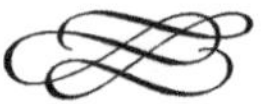

JO

"*Ofah*," I grunt in frustration when the orb rising in the middle of the circle dissipates. Rulya, Divahni, and Qayeko avoid my gaze as I take a deep breath and try again. We have been trying all morning to practice this spell, but it is me who continues to lose focus and ruin it just when the orb starts to glow a bright green shade.

Qayeko clears his throat. "It is all right, Jobaki. We shall start again," he says, trying to reassure me that I am not a complete failure. However, his efforts are futile because if I cannot even channel our shared energies into an orb of peace, how am I ever going to lead the coven as Prime? This is a simple spell to cast, which is why I chose it. We cannot even get this right.

Tibik stumbles upon our circle as he steps out into the side yard and shakes his head at us. "Why was I not invited to join this circle? It seems an egregious error to exclude the Prime from such an exercise."

"You were not home when we gathered for spell practice," I reply in a short, clipped tone. He is never interested in joining us for spell practice unless the spell we are practicing is a hex on another, or a ritual to extend our lifespan. Those are his two passions in life.

"Still," he says, coming to stand behind me, leaning over with pursed lips as he scrutinizes our setup, "you should have waited."

I blow out a steady, calming breath, trying to push away his toxic energy. I must not engage with his passing comments. He is trying to goad me into an argument, which he has successfully done twice since Alu left yesterday. The tension among the coven is at an all-time high, and I do not want our clashing viewpoints to take a toll on the other Hexrins. They do not deserve to be caught in the middle.

"I am beginning to think you do not value me as Prime of this coven, Jobaki," he says in a condescending tone. "There will be repercussions if this lack of respect continues."

An unexpected roar of laughter rips from my throat, and I blurt, "As if your power could do anything to hurt me." I do not recognize my own voice or the disdain dripping from every word. I break the circle by getting to my feet and stepping into Tibik's personal space. He is taller than me, much taller, in fact, but he is weak. Pitiful. He does not scare me with his idle threats. I press my pointer finger into his chest, letting my sharp claw push through the fabric of his tunic. "You are nothing but an insect taunting a storm cloud."

"Is that so?" he leans into my claw, towering over me in an effort to intimidate me. "Are you implying that your power is greater than mine?"

"No," I reply instantly, tilting my chin up to meet his defiant, furious gaze. "To *imply* would mean I am passively suggesting it. I am telling you directly, and in front of our coven, that your power is no match for mine, and it never will be."

He scoffs as he takes in the other members of our coven whose attention is now locked on the two of us.

"Have you forgotten the arrangement we created when we first joined together, Tibik?" I ask him. Normally, this is something I would bring up in a quiet voice, and in private, but as I have reached the end of my patience with him, I ask the question loudly.

He swallows, looking unsure of himself. The movement is subtle, but I notice it.

"What arrangement?" Divahni asks.

Then he lowers his voice as he says, "That arrangement was made long before I honed my power. I was not the Hexrin I am today."

What an incredible delusion he has created. "So you are saying you think you deserve the role of Prime? That you have earned it?"

He jerks back, looking offended. "Of course I have earned it. Otherwise, I would not still hold the title."

"You hold the title because you have yet to be challenged for it," I remind him.

He chuckles, and his chuckle grows into a loud cackle that shakes his entire body. "What are you saying?" he asks the moment the laughter fades just enough to allow him to speak. "That you wish to challenge me for the role of Prime?"

I nod. "Indeed. That is what I am saying."

The other Hexrins gasp as they get to their feet.

"Kituva Bravati?" Rulya asks both of us. *Challenge of Power.*

"Yes," I reply as Tibik protests.

"No, this is a foolish endeavor that will be a waste of everyone's time." He is afraid or in deep denial. Either way, I am looking forward to defeating him.

I shrug. "It will not be a waste of time for the coven, or the clan, to see which of us is the rightful Prime." Then I lean closer to Tibik. "Unless you are concerned you are not strong enough to emerge victorious?"

"When do you wish to hold the *Kituva Bravati?*" Qayeko asks. "We will need enough time to prepare the supplies and gather the clan."

"Excellent point, Qayeko," Tibik says with a proud grin. "Let us schedule the *Kituva Bravati* for the eve of the full moon next cycle."

"Why would we wait until the next cycle when there is a full moon this very eve?" I point out. I know why he wishes to put it off— because he knows I will beat him. I just want him to admit it.

He does not, however, because his weakness is his pride, which will be the death of him.

"It is not enough time for our coven to gather the supplies we need," Tibik says.

"That is not true," Rulya says, stunning me to silence with her reply. She has never disagreed with Tibik before. Her mouth curves up on one side as she looks at me, then adds, "We have most of the supplies already. We will just need to find something for the final phase."

"So you are saying we can hold the *Kituva Bravati* this eve?" I ask, excitement pumping through my blood at the prospect of defeating Tibik this soon.

Rulya nods. "Yes, I shall locate the supplies for the final phase while Divahni and Qayeko clear the space and alert the clan."

"Where should the event be held?" Divahni asks.

Tibik's cheeks and neck darken as he says, "There is not enough space within the village to do this. We must find another location."

I cannot let that happen. While I am confident my power could best his, I still do not trust him. If he is given time to find another location, I am certain he will do something to manipulate the space and use it to his advantage. If we have the test this eve, he will not get the chance to do so.

"No, we shall hold it this eve, on the main path of the village," I say. "Let the entire clan watch."

The younger Hexrins exchange glances of exhilaration before they rush off to tend to their respective tasks, leaving Tibik and me alone.

"You will regret this, Jobaki," he grits. "You are not courageous enough to be our Prime."

Perhaps the latter is true, but I do know he is wrong about the former. No matter what happens, I am certain I will not regret it.

* * *

As soon as the sun sets and the glow of the full moon shines through the trees, the clan gathers on either side of the main path, a crackle of anticipation filling the air as everyone's eyes are locked on Tibik and me.

Normally, any kind of ceremony or event is held at the far end of the path where the food hall is located. There is usually a meal component to our events, and the setting has adequate seating to accommodate the entire clan. But since the food hall is currently in a shambolic state and this is not an event where food is served, we are holding the *Kituva Bravati* farther down the path.

Kate uses a rope with strange markings on it to measure the distance between Tibik and me. "Twenty feet," she says with a smile.

I stare at the space, trying to decipher her meaning. "Feet? There are not ten clan members standing between us. They stand alongside the path with their feet."

Kate laughs loudly. "It's a measurement we used on Earth. Not actual feet."

"And twenty feet of distance is a good thing?" I ask.

"I don't know," she says with a shrug. Then she dangles the rope in front of me, showing off the markings. "I just made this. Isn't it cool? It's like a crude measuring tape."

Her words make no sense, but I nod, agreeing with words I have heard her say many times: "Quite cool…Kayt."

"Hey, are you sure about this?" she asks, turning to face me. "I don't want you rushing into this because you're in pain and just want some kind of release for that anger."

"But it will be such a satisfying release, no?" I reply with a smirk. Her concern is flattering, but I am not sure Kayt is aware of how long I have wanted to do this, or how easily I can defeat a male like Tibik.

"Your supplies are set up in order of the challenge phases," Rulya says at my side.

I look over her work, pleased with the organization and timeliness in which she and the other Hexrins put this together. "Are you sure you are comfortable explaining the rules to the clan?"

Her smile is wide as she nods eagerly. "Yes, I am."

"Very well," I tell her, gesturing for her to step into the center of the path.

She does and clears her throat. Her posture takes on a kind of authoritative grace that I have not seen before. Rulya is looking forward to this entire event, it seems.

"Attention, Clan!" she shouts, and a hush falls over the crowd.

Kayt gives me a hug before rushing off to find her mate. My heart squeezes at the thought of Alu cheering me on from somewhere among the clan, but that is merely a daydream I must push away as I cannot let the thought of her, with her thick, sumptuous lips and muscular thighs, interrupt my focus.

Then I remember how badly she wanted this for me. She was thrilled at the prospect of me standing up to Tibik and being courageous enough to claim the role of Prime. She even helped me visualize what it would feel like to take that step and lead the clan, and the feeling was glorious.

If I succeed this eve, I imagine it would make her proud. But I must succeed first.

"We gather beneath the light of the moon for a most sacred purpose," Rulya continues. "The *Kituva Bravati* is a meeting of two seasoned Hexrins, and a test to see whose power is dominant. There are four phases to this test. These phases must occur in the following order: *lunwanavi,* which is telekinesis; *lunwopiivyo,* or teleportation; *killyaveh,* as in elemental control; and finally *pohrrixo,* also known as necromancy."

I have spent a significant amount of time practicing all of these skills. The only one I have had some trouble with is the final phase, necromancy. The concept of reanimating the dead has always turned my stomach, so I have been hesitant to work with that area of magic, but I am certain I remember the steps I learned at the Hexrin academy.

"Our participating Hexrins, Jobaki and Tibik, must complete each phase before moving on to the next," Rulya says. "If one or both are unable to complete a phase, they are immediately disqualified and the title of Prime shall be awarded to the victor. If both are able to complete all four phases, then it will come down to time. Whichever Hexrin is able to finish first shall assume the role of Prime. Interruptions or participation of any kind from spectators is prohibited."

Rulya turns toward Tibik. "Hexrin Tibik, are you ready?"

"Ready," he replies, shaking out his limbs and cracking his knuckles.

Then she turns toward me. "Hexrin Jobaki, are you ready?"

I feel a familiar tingle in the tips of my fingers, my blood pumping with centuries of resentment and fury. This is a role I was meant to claim.

Nodding, I lift my palms in front of my chest. "I am ready."

CHAPTER 17

ALU

_I_ had no plans to return to the village after what happened between me and Jo. But Mek has not returned to the caves, and it has been an entire day. He is never away from me this long. Something must have happened.

Or, the more likely scenario, he made his way back to Jo shortly after leaving the caves and has remained at her side ever since.

Kate and Niro left for the village early this morning to look for Mek, and also to add decorations to their new home in the village. They told me they would send a comm if they locate Mek, and if I do not hear from them, to fly down to the village whenever I am ready. They gave me the option of not going at all, promising they would look for him until they returned to the caves tomorrow morning.

So it is not required for me to travel to the village. I could remain here and hope Mek returns. But the caves are far too quiet with no one else here, and it is possible that Kate and Niro do not know all the places in the village to look for Mek. He is very good at hiding when he wants to.

It does not take long to fly from the caves to the village, and when I land on the patch of grass outside the forest, part of me wishes Jo were here to greet me with her large, golden eyes shining with adoration as her short legs bring her straight into my open arms. However, that is not what occurs, and I sigh heavily as I trudge through the trees and thickets, knowing that day will never come.

When I emerge onto the main path, I am immediately taken aback by the crowd of people lining the edges on either side, whispering quietly to each other as their attention is heavily focused on whatever is happening in the center.

I spot Kate's fiery red hair right away, and slowly make my way to her and Niro. "What is this? Did you locate Mek?" I ask when I reach them.

Kate scrunches her freckled nose and her lips curve into a frown. "No, sorry. No sign of him yet."

I peer over the heads of a few people standing in front of me, but I still cannot get a clear view of what everyone is watching.

"Kate, what is this?" I ask again.

"Oh, Jo and Tibik are about to kick off something called the *Kituva Bravati*," she explains in a hushed tone. "It's a challenge between Hexrins fighting for the role of Prime."

"Jo is battling Tibik for the Prime title?" I ask, shocked by Kate's words, but I suppose I should not be. It has been Jo's dream for quite some time. I am glad she is finally chasing it. Watching her come undone in my arms as she faced her fear of stepping into the role was one of the most profound moments of my lifetime. I have never witnessed anything quite as beautiful, and I am certain I never will again.

I grab Kate's hand and pull her through the crowd until there is no one else in front of us.

"Alussanai, what are you doing?" Niro grumbles from somewhere behind me.

Niro follows and stands behind Kate, his arms wrapped around her middle.

"I am about to watch my mate fight a disgraceful male for a role that was always meant to be hers," I explain, my eyes finally landing on Jo. "I cannot do that without my family at my side."

"Did you say your *mate?*" Kate asks, lifting her brow.

I shoot her a skeptical glance. "Did I?" If I did, it was certainly not intentional, but I also do not feel the need to argue with Kate. The word repeats in my mind as I watch Jo lift her palms in front of her heart, her gigantic, soft heart, and I suddenly see how well the label fits.

Jo is my mate.

She is! my draxilio shouts. *Why have you denied it for so long? You fool!*

Of course she is. It seems so silly that I ever denied it, or resisted the possibility of it, when the truth could not be clearer. Jo is the other half of my soul. She is the air I breathe.

No one has made me feel the way she does. It is not just the sex either. Certainly that is incomparable, but it is more than that. She cares for me in a way no one has. My lack of fear scares Jo, but it comes from a place of adoration. She worries I will hurt myself, or that something will happen, and she will lose me. It is not that my pursuits will embarrass her, as has been the case with my brothers. No, Jo's worries come from a place of love.

She…loves me.

Or *did* she love me, but no longer does? Surely, if she did love me, she would not have ended our relationship.

The crowd cheers wildly, and the noise breaks through my thoughts. "What has happened?" I ask Kate, gently elbowing her side.

"Hey," she whines, even though I am certain I did not hurt her. "I can't believe you missed that. Jo just completed the telekinesis phase by taking a giant log and turning it into tiny wood chips using just her mind."

I spot the pile of wood chips in front of Jo, and vow to keep my focus on my mate during the rest of the event. She is probably not aware I am here, but I shall support her with my whole heart nonetheless.

"What is next?" I ask, my gaze darting between Jo and Tibik. I do not trust that male. He lacks the honor required to be Prime.

"Um, I think this one is teleportation," Kate says. "Phase two."

Tibik moves first, a blur surrounding his body before he disappears in a blink, only to reappear on top of Nalba's roof, then in the center of the path, and finally back to his original position. Jo responds with the same blur Tibik had, and disappears from her spot, then lands in the middle of the path, then high above in a nearby tree, then on top of Chloe and Varrek's home, and finally in her original position, but her movement from one spot to the next seemed much faster than Tibik's.

The crowd howls as soon as Jo returns to her spot, and I get the sense that the entire clan is rooting for Jo to best Tibik. It makes me wonder why Tibik is still around at all. Clearly, he is not wanted here, is a terrible leader to the coven, and has caused harm in the past. What purpose does he serve?

Kate leans next to my ear. "The next phase is elemental control," she whispers as a hush falls over the crowd.

I have not had the pleasure of watching Jo practice any of these skills, and it feels as if she was too shy to show me just how powerful she is. I wish that had not been the case, but perhaps, once this is over and she takes over as Prime, she would be willing to show me more.

Tibik begins this phase by creating a glowing orange orb between his palms, his hands spreading farther apart as the orb expands. Moving one hand away, he turns his other palm toward the sky and blows on the orb hovering just above it. The orb transforms, the air from his lungs feeding into it, until he brings his arm back and throws the orb toward the center of the path. It lands as a ball of fire in the dirt; the flames crackling as they consume the chips of wood Jo made during phase one.

Jo's gaze turns steely as she strides toward the fire that is now widening in the center of the path. The crowd gasps as the flames grow, but Jo's expression holds no concern at all. She lifts her chin, raises her right hand while spreading her fingers, and brings her hand down swiftly, as if scratching her claws against a rough surface.

Water streams onto the path from above, but only as far wide as the fire reaches. Nothing else is touched by a drop. The flames die within the span of a heartbeat, as Jo sweeps her hand across the center of the path, turning the charred, damaged wood ash into tiny sparks that float into the evening sky.

A strong gust of wind whips through the village, leaving the clan shivering with bewildered expressions on their faces. Tibik smiles as he condenses the wind into a narrow path that he makes smaller and smaller until a funnel cloud appears in his upturned palm. When his eyes land on Jo, he smiles wickedly and flicks the funnel cloud toward her. The moment it leaves his palm, it grows into the size of most of the homes in the village, and it is suddenly barreling toward her.

I do not breathe. I do not think. I just clench my fists as I watch this unfold, hoping Jo knows how to respond.

Moments before the funnel cloud reaches her, she raises her pointer finger and drags it across the dirt in front of her, leaving a clear line through the soil. That is where the funnel cloud dies. It is as if Jo created an invisible wall, and the funnel cloud evaporated as soon as it hit it.

There is only one element that has not been used in this phase, and that is earth. Jo's eyes fall closed as she extends her arms in front of her, palms facing up. I feel the air change the deeper Jo's focus becomes, and when a hint of a smile appears on her face, she curls her fingers into her palms and yanks her arms inward.

The ground shifts beneath Tibik's feet, and he instantly loses his balance as the dirt and rock and grass he was standing on is pulled closer to Jo. He scrambles back up, but she does it again, and he tumbles to the ground on his hands and knees.

Jo does this three more times, during which the roar of the crowd gets louder and louder, laughter filling the air when Tibik tries to get to his feet and cannot.

Eventually, Jo drops her hands to her sides and her eyes flutter open. She is lethal, my tiny witch. I have never wanted to run my tongue over her skin more than I do right now.

One of the younger Hexrins with the long, curly maroon hair, steps into the middle of the path with her hands raised. "It is now time for phase four: *pohrrixo*."

"Necromancy," Kate whispers in translation.

"This is widely known among Hexrins as the most difficult skill a witch can master," the young Hexrin continues. "Tibik and Jobaki have each been given a dead *xoobawya* fish pulled from the cold box in the back of the food hall. These fish were originally caught at the small cabin by the lake, quite a long distance from here. They have been dead for many moon cycles. It is Tibik's and Jobaki's responsibility to bring these fish back to life before our eyes."

Tibik and Jo take a few steps toward the small tables set up in front of them, where the fish are lying in the center.

Several moments pass, and Tibik and Jo have the same look of intense focus, despite no changes to the fish in front of them. Each Hexrin has their eyes closed, and an open palm turned down over the fish as they struggle to reanimate them.

Eventually, I hear several oohs coming from the members of the clan to my left, and I turn to discover the fish on Tibik's table wiggling frantically.

People start clapping when Tibik's fish opens and closes its mouth, and my heart sinks.

No. No, no, no. Tibik cannot win this phase. It will mean he wins everything, and Jo will be forced to serve him as Prime of their coven.

"Finish this, Jo!" I shout without thinking. But I am powerless to do anything to help her beyond cheering, so that is what I do. "You can do this!"

Her eyes open, and immediately find mine in the crowd. She smiles, tears threatening to spill onto her cheeks. I put my hands over my heart and nod, trying to communicate wordlessly that I am proud of her no matter the outcome.

She takes a deep breath, shakes out her arms, and returns her focus to the fish.

Still, nothing happens.

When Jo's posture changes, I take it as a good sign, grabbing Kate's hand excitedly. "This is it!" I say, jumping in place. My tiny witch is about to become Prime.

Without warning, Jo collapses onto the table, sending the still-dead fish flying behind her before she tumbles awkwardly to the ground. It is then I notice the color of her skin—a paler, sickly shade of gold that continues to fade at an alarming rate. Her eyes widen with fright as she clutches at her chest. She turns her head toward Tibik, and the rest of the crowd follows suit.

Tibik is doing this to her. He stands with a menacing sneer, his arm outstretched with his hand curled inward as if clutching a ball.

Whispers from the clan turn to shouts as people demand to know what is happening. The three younger Hexrins look between each other, clearly not knowing what is going on or how to proceed.

Though it is clear to me what Tibik is doing. He is draining the life from Jo's body right in front of us as part of this final phase. There is no telling whether he plans to bring her back to life once he stops her heart.

And I…cannot move. My chest tightens as I watch Jo's small frame continue to wither as she lies in the dirt, gasping for the breath being sucked out of her lungs, and it feels as if I am frozen in place. Every cell in my body feels as if it is screaming.

Go! Stop this now! Save our mate!

My draxilio even wants me to end this and save Jo, but, despite the overwhelming desperation to run toward Tibik and sever his head, or to shift and burn Tibik's bones to ash, or a number of other scenarios in which I defeat Tibik and save Jo, my palms grow sweaty, my heartbeat begins to race, and my limbs become numb.

Time feels as if it is slowing and speeding up at once, and a chill races down my spine as Jo's eyes close.

It is only when her entire body stills that realization hits.

This is fear.

I am experiencing genuine, debilitating fear at the prospect of losing my mate.

My mind is not broken. In fact, it is healing.

A stillness washes over me as my purpose becomes clear. It is immediately followed by the kind of rage that can only be felt by a draxilio whose mate has been threatened. It is a fury I have never experienced, and keeping Tibik in my sights, I lean into it with all that I am.

My feet dig into the soft soil as I charge Tibik. A steady and thunderous growl is pulled from my chest and fills the air, and I feel my body loosen ahead of the transformation. My draxilio purrs in delight as I let her take over. She is primal and brutal and wants nothing more than to slice her claws through Tibik's organs and spill his blood all over the main path.

Tibik spots me just before the shift begins, a flash of terror in his gaze as he turns his body toward me. His fingers uncurl and a purple orb appears in his palm.

It is the only warning I get before he turns his palm toward me and shoots it toward my chest.

CHAPTER 18

JO

*A*ir.

More air.

I need more.

It is the only thing on my mind as Tibik releases his hold on me, and I gasp for breath. My hands claw at my neck and chest, and my mouth opens wide as I continue to wheeze, desperately seeking the return of my normal breathing pattern.

"Niro! Nooo!" I hear Kayt scream.

I roll onto my side and watch in horror as Nee-roh pushes through the crowd and charges Tibik. It is not until after Tibik sends a deep crimson orb into his chest, sending him flying into the forest, that I discover why.

It is because Tibik is holding Alu's unconscious body inside a purple orb, the orb of immobility, high above the ground.

I struggle to get to my feet, still weakened from what Tibik attempted. He let his ego guide his hand, and he tried to suck the life from my body before he reanimated me. It would have been an impressive way to win the *Kituva Bravati* and secure the title of Prime, but Alu must have interfered and stolen his focus, because now he is holding her inside the orb as he turns it around slowly for the crowd to see, and I am left here, unattended.

How foolish of him.

Suddenly, the argument I had with Alu no longer seems important. She is clumsy—so what? She is not someone who intentionally tries to hurt people. Her destruction of the food hall was an accident, and I unleashed the anger I felt toward Tibik upon her instead.

I must apologize and win her back. But first, I must rescue her from the orb of immobility before Tibik tries anything sinister.

Closing my eyes, I focus my power in the center of my palms, where it always originates, and lock onto the orb using a protection spell that I quietly recite under my breath.

Tibik feels my intrusion and starts laughing maniacally.

"You think you can win this one?" he shouts. "I almost killed you once, Jobaki. Do not make me do it again."

I step toward Tibik, keeping my tread light and my body still. He is still not looking at me, and I do not want that to change. His focus remains on Alu.

"Let her go, Tibik," I say, my voice still a low rasp. "This is between the two of us, and who will become Prime. Alu is not part of it."

"Is she not?" he asks with a snicker, turning the orb so that Alu is facing me. Her eyes are open, but there is nothing behind them. The orb of immobility traps the body of a person while sending them into a state of unconsciousness. She knows not what happens right now. "This draxilio has invaded our village, our coven, and she has kept you from focusing on what should be your only priority—your magic."

"That is not true," I bark back. "She invaded nothing. I invited her here." I have taken six steps toward Tibik, but the distance that remains is still too great for my liking. My protection spell is a temporary shield around her body inside the orb. I do not know how long it will last, or what he plans to do with her once it fades.

Finally, Tibik's eyes meet mine. "It is such a shame," he says, shaking his head. "When we began working together, I saw incredible potential in you, Jobaki." His face twists into a look of disgust. "But you have been a catastrophic disappointment."

His opinion of me means nothing at this point, given what he has already attempted, and the only reason I am paying any attention to his words is to determine what his next move is.

He lets out a weary sigh, then sends a crimson orb barreling toward me. I block it just in time, but it is enough to release my shield around Alu.

"Say goodbye to your plaything," he taunts. Then he awakens her from inside the orb. Her body jerks as she looks around and slams her fists against the barrier, trying to free herself from his hold.

Her eyes meet mine, and the panic in them threatens to send me to my knees. Out of nowhere, a horrid stench hits my nose, and it is as if parts of me suddenly awaken—parts that I did not even know existed. I look around the path for the source of the smell, and my gaze is dragged back to Alu.

The scent comes from her. It is fear.

Alu is experiencing fear.

My heartbeat quickens as her fear scent fills my lungs, and it is only when I feel wetness dripping down my fingers that I realize my claws have pierced the skin of my palms. Is Tibik doing this to me? When a wave of lightheadedness causes me to stumble, I realize it is not Tibik at all.

It is the tether. My soul has recognized Alu as my mate, my reason for living. My inara.

Tibik continues laughing as he uses his free hand to twist and pull at the air, causing Alu's eyes to roll back in her head and her claws to scratch at her throat.

"No!" I shout as her body goes limp inside the orb.

He is killing her. It is the same spell he used to pull the breath from my lungs, and he is doing it now to Alu, my fearless draxilio.

A blood-curdling scream fills the air, the echo bouncing off the trees, and it is only when my feet leave the ground that I realize the sound comes from me. A bright orange glow surrounds my entire body as I float higher. Tears blur my vision, but I feel no pain.

Only power.

Pure, impenetrable power shoots out of my every pore as I bring my palms in front of my chest. I focus on the terror I saw in Alu's eyes right before her body went limp, and I let vengeance fill my lungs as I slowly breathe in and out.

My eyes land on Tibik, and his mouth hangs open as he watches me hover above him, magic radiating from deep within my body. Our entire relationship was built on how he could manipulate me into giving him my power.

It is time I take it back.

I close the distance between my palms, pressing them together before I push them apart in a downward sweeping motion that sends me hurtling back down. The moment my feet connect with the ground, a deep crack forms in the land between my feet, shaking the entire village. But I do not care about the state of the village, or if the entire planet of Oluura crumbles to dust. I only care about Alu, and whether she will survive. I need her to survive.

If she does not, it will be from Tibik's doing.

Slamming my hand over the crack, a bolt of orange light shoots from my fingertips and races toward Tibik through the soil.

It is the strongest surge of power I have ever felt, and it should frighten me, especially when I do not turn away from it. But it does not. The deeper I lean into the power, the more it feels right.

I feel it rip through the ground as if the bolt is an extension of my body, and when it hits Tibik, I revel in the feel of it slicing through his insides. It burns his muscles, cuts through bone, and I cannot help but smile as his organs shut down one by one. Then his heartbeat slows and eventually comes to a stop.

My gaze lands on Alu, and I race to her side as fast as my feet will take me. I kneel next to her crumpled form lying in the dirt as tears stain my cheeks. "Alu!" I cry out, gently turning her onto her back.

Nee-roh, Kayt, and Varrek quickly surround us with matching looks of dread.

"She'll be okay," Kayt says, her tone distant and unconvincing.

"Alussanai!" Nee-roh shouts, shaking her shoulders.

"Be careful!" Kayt yells as she pulls his hands away. "If she's badly injured, you're going to make it worse."

I do not even know if Alu is breathing until a pained groan escapes her lips. She opens her eyes slowly, her gaze moving around to each face until it finally lands on mine. "Jo," she says, her voice a scratchy whisper, her entire body shivering.

In the background, I hear relieved sighs from Kayt and Nee-roh, but I do not pay attention to them. Alu is alive and there is love in her eyes when she looks at me.

"Alu!" I say in a choked sob as I press her palm against my cheek. *"Vana kiyle tu benof charchery vunup xi hulliya bo wqikiva. Kukuvai qpi mussaw kwe dinl sah ul nuzilba."*

Her eyes water upon hearing the Sufoian phrase draxilio mothers would say to their children. Then she smiles so wide, light shines in her eyes.

"Are you hurt? Do you wish to sit up?" Quickly, I look over her body and do not see any visible injuries or wounds, but it is possible Tibik caused internal damage.

"Jo," she whispers again. "My Jo."

I cover her face with light kisses as I continue to cry. I cannot believe I almost lost her right after learning she is the one who I am meant to spend my life with.

She groans again, trying, and failing, to push herself up.

"Let us help you," I tell her. Nee-roh and I support her back as she pulls her upper body forward, and eventually we get her settled into a seated position.

She rubs a hand on the back of her neck as she looks around, confused. "What happened?" she asks. Then, in the span of a heartbeat, her eyes widen as she grabs my wrist. "Did you win? Are you Prime Hexrin of the coven?"

I had forgotten all about the *Kituva Bravati* the moment Tibik trapped Alu inside that orb. Although, I suppose, since Tibik is dead, the role is now mine for the taking, despite not having completed the final phase. I never did bring that fish back from the dead.

Realizing how little the title matters to me, I take Alu's face in my hands and press my forehead against hers. "I do not care about anything but you, Alu. You are my mate. My inara. I felt the tether the moment I smelled your fear. Your fear! It was there."

She chuckles as she wraps her hands around my wrists. "When you fell, I did not know what was happening to me," she whispers, "I was so afraid of losing you."

"I thought I had lost you too," I admit. "It was the worst moment of my life."

She presses her lips against mine, and her taste eases the panic that still twists my insides. The kiss is somewhat clumsy, and our tears continue to fall as our tongues swirl around each other, but I do not care. Alu is alive, and she is mine.

Or…is she? I suppose we have not addressed that yet.

I pull back to look at her and take a deep breath. "Alussanai, will you be my mate?" I ask.

She chuckles as she peppers my cheeks with featherlight kisses. "Yes," she says, pulling me down on top of her. "Yes, I will be your mate."

"Oh, wait," she says, her sudden hesitation filling me with worry. "Are you certain there is room for me in the coven house? That is where you wish to live, yes?"

"Well, yes," I tell her. "I will need to spend the majority of my time there."

"Of course there is room," Rulya replies happily.

It is then that I notice the entire clan has gathered around us in a tight circle, watching as we roll around in the dirt. Alu and I sit up, offering awkward smiles to our audience. Rulya and Qayeko pull us to our feet, and Qayeko adds, "We would be honored to have you in our home, Alu. Your open spirit is good for the coven."

"Truly?" she asks, hope swirling in her eyes. I suppose it is my fault that Alu is surprised by the Hexrins' reactions. I did a terrible job of making her feel welcome in the coven house. That is a mistake I must rectify immediately.

"Truly," I add. "You brighten every space you enter, inara. Our home is yours," then I add, "if you do not mind living with a coven of

Hexrins." She has an entire cottage to herself, and I cannot imagine she is looking forward to giving that up to move into a crowded house with a group of witches.

"I just want to be where you are," she says, bringing my hand to her lips and kissing my palm.

"Good," I tell her, "because I am never letting you go again."

CHAPTER 19

ALU

I expect the clan to keep us on the main path with their questions for Jo about how she defeated Tibik, which I am not totally clear on, or more about her magical powers, but they do not. After the other coven members tell me I am welcome to move in with them, the clan steps aside, giving Jo and me more room than we need to leave the path and head back to the coven house.

Perhaps they are afraid of her.

If that is the case, then it is about time. From what I have heard from Kate, and the little I have witnessed myself while being in the village, Jobaki was mostly invisible. She let Tibik lead the coven, and she did her best to fade into the shadows.

That is not her destiny, however. Jo is meant to rule. I do not understand why no one else could see this before now, but to me, her calling has been obvious from the very first moment.

Now, though, it is undeniable in the way she carries herself. There is a newfound ease in the way she moves that makes me proud to be her mate.

Her *mate*.

We have found our mate! We shall never be alone again. My draxilio releases a steady purr inside my chest, showing the unwavering state of her elation.

I am hers, and she is mine. Neither of us thought it was possible, but we are here, practically floating as we head toward the Hexrin house to have the mating ceremony and solidify our bond.

"What is involved in this ceremony?" I ask, my gaze locked on the sway of her hips in front of me.

"The moment we reach release, we must exchange a bite," she explains. "It does not have to be at the same time, just whenever you feel you are close to coming, I must bite you hard enough to break the skin, and you must return that bite."

"What happens after the bite?"

She sighs dreamily. "Then we will get very tired and fall asleep. And when we wake, our minds will be eternally linked."

"You will hear my thoughts?"

"Yes," she says with an amused chuckle. "You will hear mine, as well."

"Hmm. What does a Prime Hexrin think about during the day?"

"I cannot speak for other Primes, but I know I will be thinking about your lips," she says, her cheeks darkening. "Or your hands."

"My hands?" I ask, surprised. Of all the parts she could appreciate, she chooses my hands?

"They are magnificent hands."

I lift my free hand in front of my face to examine it. "They look like normal draxilio hands to me."

Jo throws the front door open and pulls me inside. She shoves me against the back of the door and attacks my neck with her lips. "It is not how they look," she says in a breathy moan between kisses, "it is how you use them."

Now I understand.

We tear at each other's clothing as we climb the steps to her bedroom. By the time we reach it, I am down to just a shirt, and Jo is wearing one boot. She kicks it off and the boot flies across the room. The moment my shirt is off, I toss it into the corner with the boot.

I stalk toward her, and her lips part as she steps back, maintaining the distance between us. Her brow lifts as she continues backing from me, a challenge, it seems.

"I *will* catch you, tiny witch. Do not even think about running."

When her back hits the wall, her hands cover her breasts, kneading the tips into hardened, dark-gold points that make my mouth water.

I run my nose along the length of her throat when I reach her, and place my palms on either side of her head, caging her in. "Mmm," I groan as I shove my nose into her hair. "Your scent. I want to breathe it in for the rest of time."

Jo splays a hand on my lower back and pulls me flush against her body. "You will," she says just before she crushes her lips to mine. It is a bruising, punishing kiss, as the anguish we both felt tonight pours from our lips. She uses her fangs to nip at the tip of my tongue, and I let out a needy, desperate moan as my hips buck against her.

Her breaths come out in short pants against my cheek as I let one hand drift down her body, avoiding her breasts entirely and trailing the center of her chest.

She whimpers in protest. "Stop teasing me."

My claw traces a lazy circle around her belly button. "You want my hand, tiny witch?"

"Yesss," she hisses, reaching for my wrist. But I pull it away.

"I want to hear it again," I whisper against her neck.

"H-hear what?" she pants.

"The Trovilian term for fated mate. You said it earlier. Say it again."

My fingers trail down the lower part of her stomach and stop just before they reach the lips of her cunt.

"Inara," she moans, rocking her hips forward to meet my hand.

"Yes, that is it," I reply, running a finger down her swollen seam. She is already so wet.

"Ah!" she cries out as I push my finger inside her tight heat.

"And what am I?" I ask, dropping my head until I can flick my tongue against her nipple.

She groans as she throws her head back. "My inara."

Agreeing, I take her nipple into my mouth and suck hard. I slide another finger inside her cunt, her juices dripping down my hand.

Her hands tangle in my hair as she meets each thrust of my hand with her hips. Soon, I feel her body quiver and her k'billita pulse against my fingers. She is close.

Pressing the flat of my tongue against her nipple, it starts to vibrate.

"Alu, yes—ah!" she cries out as she comes, her entire body quaking against me.

I shove my face into the crook of her neck and bite down until I taste blood. Then I run my tongue across the wound until the bleeding stops.

Her chest continues to heave as she looks up at me with swollen lips and dazed eyes. Pride fills my chest at the sight of my mate thoroughly sexed. I did that.

She chuckles through short, panting breaths as she ducks beneath my arm and drops to her knees, pushing me until my back hits the wall.

Then Jo shoves her face between my thighs and lavishes my cunt with her tongue. She alternates between sucking on my lips and stroking her tongue into the depths of my core, and turning my breaths ragged in an instant as I try to keep up with all the sensations shooting through my body.

"Faster," I command when she starts swirling the tip of her tongue in a tight circle just inside my cunt, swiping along my *avuno*. "Yes, yes," I whimper as she picks up the pace. I run my claws along her scalp and then rest my hand at the back of her head, keeping her in place as I arch my back off the wall. My body is as tight as a bowstring, and Jo has me on the verge of snapping.

Soon, her tongue is twisting and dipping inside me at a pace that does not seem possible, by draxilio or Trovilian standards, but then again, this is my tiny witch, and she tends to break barriers.

My scream fills the room, maybe even the whole house, as I am thrown over the edge. And within a breath, I feel Jo's fangs sink into the fleshy part of my inner thigh. The sting of the bite lengthens my release, and I find I am still pumping my hips against her face shamelessly as she cleans the blood from the bite.

She stands on shaky legs, and I find mine are just as wobbly as she takes my hand and pulls me onto the bed. I do not even get under the blankets before my muscles relax and sleep pulls me under.

* * *

Wake up, my beautiful inara.

Jo's words meet my ears, pulling me from the deepest slumber I can remember having. I smile when her face comes into view and pull her against me. She smells so good, even now. I want nothing more than to lift her above my head and have her ride my face until she screams.

We should get up and start the day, but that sounds like a wonderful plan for later, she replies, but…not out loud.

My eyes fly open as I turn toward her.

She smiles, and without moving her mouth, she says, *This is strange to you, yes? Do not worry, I have heard most mates adjust quickly.*

I go to speak, but instantly snap my lips shut and focus on opening my mind to her.

You do not need to do that; she sends through our mental link. *I am already here.*

Wow! I was not expecting it to be like this, I send back.

Uncertainty tightens her features. *Do you not like it?*

No, I love it! Now I can be with you all the time.

I feel her love and warmth through our link. *I love it too,* she sends back.

Someone knocks softly on our door. "Yes?" Jo says.

A high-pitched caw fills the air the moment Rulya opens the door a crack. "Mek!" I shout, and he turns on his side to fly through the narrow opening, before landing between Jo and me on the bed.

Rulya giggles as she leans against the door. "I was told he was missing."

"Yes," I reply. "He left the caves, and I did not know where he went. Though I assumed he came back here."

Jo strokes the feathers on his head, and he leans into her touch.

A moment later, Qayeko races into the room, gasping for breath. "Jobaki, you are needed outside. Now."

"Qayeko, what has happened?" Jo demands.

The side of Qayeko's mouth curves up. "*Pohrrixo.*"

"What?" I ask, confused.

Jo does not answer. Instead, she leaps off the bed and grabs the closest items of clothing she can reach and throws them on. I follow suit before racing down the stairs and out the front door.

I skid to a stop on the main path directly behind Jo as she mutters, "Oh, goddess. What have I done?"

Marching through the center of the village is a group of warriors. No, not warriors. I am not sure what they are, exactly. From the looks of them, they are…not well. Their skin is a pale, sickly greenish gray, with a translucent quality to it. Deep black circles surround their eyes. Their lips are also black, and though they are wearing clothes—scraps of clothes, really—I can see their bones through their skin. Not in the sense that they are thin enough for their bones to be visible, their bodies are heavily muscled, but when the light hits them in certain spots, I can see the skeleton beneath. Though it is difficult to notice anything beyond the long and gaping wounds that cover their bodies.

They are terrifying. And their glowing white eyes are locked on Jo.

"What is this?" I ask, not knowing if I need to shift into my draxilio and burn them where they stand, or if this is something the Hexrins are used to dealing with.

Varrek and his crew of warriors emerge from the training ground behind us, their weapons at the ready.

"No, Varrek," Jo says, waving her hands frantically as she places herself between Varrek and the gray wounded creatures approaching. "I can take care of this. I promise you."

He looks between Jo and the group approaching. "You know who they are? And what they want?"

She sighs heavily. "Yes, I think I do."

"Jo!" Kayt shouts. "What the fuck is going on?"

"They are mine," Jo says in a solemn tone. "When I sent a crack through the ground last eve, I believe I awakened them."

"Awakened?" I repeat the word, not understanding.

Jo turns to me and scrubs a hand down her face. "Yes. I, uh, I believe I have woken the dead."

EPILOGUE

JO

A WEEK LATER...

I knew becoming Prime Hexrin would be stressful in the beginning, but I was not anticipating such a massive undertaking. However, I suppose I am to blame for my current level of stress. Not every Prime is forced to care for a group of undead Vi-kings, as Kayt described them, upon stepping into the role.

"Ri Huna," one of the undead Vi-kings mutters as he kneels at my feet. It means "My Queen," and I hear it no less than a hundred times each day. They also follow me everywhere I go. Even now, as I am at a table in the food hall—the part that is still functional despite the repairs needed—looking through an old spell book, they sit at a nearby table, watching me intently.

Though I suppose it is better than it was. The first few days after they arrived were miserable. We could not figure out where they came from or what language they spoke, so communication was limited to a handful of words, grunts, and over-the-top gestures.

By day four, Nee-roh's brother, Koo-li, was able to send his scrapper, Zey-dah, to the village, and she used an advanced screen pad to determine they are an ancient alien race from a planet called Daxaev II that was destroyed centuries ago.

Zey-dah returned the following day with ear translators for the undead Vi-kings with our languages programmed in, and the members of the clan have been going to Kaiva's med room to have our language chips updated with the universal language of Daxaev II.

Being able to speak with them is an improvement, certainly, but now I must decide what to do with them. I found a spell to reverse the reanimation, but that seems cruel. Even though I was not responsible for their original deaths, I do not want their second deaths on my shoulders. I am still struggling with the knowledge that I killed Tibik, so I am not inclined to add seven undead Vi-kings to that list.

"I am sorry," I say to the undead warrior at my feet. "I do not remember your name. Could you please tell me again?"

"Onem, Ri Huna."

"Oh-nem," I repeat. "Thank you for your continued attention, but I assure you I am not in need of anything."

He does not rise. He does not move. He just keeps staring at me with those unsettling white eyes.

I spot Aye-vah walking past the food hall and an idea pops into my head. "Um, perhaps Aye-vah could take a look at that gash on your neck, yes?"

Aye-vah smiles brightly when hears her name called, but her face falls when she sees it was me. I do not take it personally. I know this is because she finds the undead males unsettling and does not want to touch their strange, translucent skin.

"Aye-vah!" I call out, gesturing for her to come over.

"Hi, Jo," she says, nodding in greeting to the male at my feet.

"This is Oh-nem, and I believe he is in need of a healer," I tell her, pointing at the gash running down the side of his neck. It is not bleeding, but it is open and not pleasant to look at.

"Um, okay, Onem," Aye-vah says with a tight smile. "Follow me. I'll get you all fixed up."

Oh-nem looks torn as Aye-vah leads him away from me, as if stepping out of my immediate vicinity will cause him physical pain. I half expect the rest of the undead to run along after him, but they do not leave the table near me.

I am back, Alu sends, moments before she comes into view. She is carrying a large sack of belongings from the cottage.

She takes a seat across from me at the table as she shows me the contents of the bag: a few blankets, the pillows that Mek turned into a nest, and a sealed jar of tibbi. *That is all?* I send. *Everything else was destroyed?*

Yes, she replies with a sadness I wish I could ease. *Either destroyed when the undead awakened, or when the rubble that was left fell over the edge of the cliff and into the pool.*

I am sorry I did not tell you about the cluster when I discovered it. I send to her. *I was worried you would be eager to feed it like you did with the feathered reptilian and it would swallow you whole.*

She chuckles through our link. *That does sound like something I would be inclined to do. I am not angry with you, my mate. You were merely trying to keep me and Mek safe.*

It seems the dark energy cluster I felt near Alu's cottage *was* the undead Vi-kings. They were buried far beneath the surface, but when I sent a crack through the ground, it brought them back to life and provided a clear path for them to join us above ground. They followed the crack right to us.

"Ri Huna," another of the Vi-kings, I think his name is Koh-dram, says as he kneels at my feet with his chin dipped.

Fah, I just want to spend time with you. Alone, I send to Alu.

She nods enthusiastically. *You have not found a spell that will help them? Or free them?*

Not yet, I reply.

"Ugh, she's so lucky," I overhear one of the newer human females whisper from a few tables behind me. I think her name is Eye-riss. "Must be nice to have a bunch of jacked dudes offer to be your slave."

"Ew, you want those zombies following you around?" the female next to her asks. Ann-ah, I think her name is. The one who helps Krahn bake the junasii bread.

"Yeah, look at them," Eye-riss replies.

"Oh, I'm looking," Ann-ah says sarcastically. "I see bones and open wounds. Yum."

"Well, I see thick veins covering their forearms and muscles bursting out of the furs they wear," Eye-riss adds.

Ann-ah scoffs. "There are several members of the clan who are covered in muscles. I'm certain they'd worship the ground you walk on."

Eye-riss lets out a sigh. "I don't know. There's just something about these guys…"

Did you hear that? I send to Alu. *The one called Eye-riss wishes the undead Vi-kings treated her as their queen.*

Humans are so strange, Alu sends back.

I nod, agreeing, as I flip through several pages in the spell book until I find what I am looking for. *Found it.*

What is it?

A transference spell, I reply. *It will not solve all our problems with them, but it will give us some much-needed time alone.*

I feel the heat in Alu's gaze as it drifts over my lips and down my neck. *Whatever it takes. Do it.*

Closing my eyes, I lift my palms in front of my chest. I feel the dark energy that was so consuming near Alu's cottage but is now much duller and less ominous. These males were hoping to be reanimated and freed. I now know that *secco oss vun* means *let us out.* For what purpose, I do not know.

But they do not seem dangerous, so that is enough of a comfort to me.

I quietly recite the spell as I turn their energy over in my hands, feeling the rough edges and the thick weight of it, before lifting my palms over my shoulder and tossing the energy behind me.

"Whoa," I hear Eye-riss mutter. "Did you guys feel that? Was that an earthquake?"

When I look at the table of undead Vi-kings, their gazes have left me and are now boring into Eye-riss's soft, round face. They stand, and together they march to her table and kneel at her feet.

"Ri Huna," they say in unison.

"U-um, hi," Eye-riss replies, somewhat nervous, but mostly giddy.

Shall we return home? I ask Alu, sending her images of the new *noogatohro* Nalba made especially for Alu and me as a mating gift.

Alu stumbles to her feet, knocking the bag off the table onto the dirt. *Yes,* she sends, the voice inside my head full of longing. She races around the table and lifts me into her arms before taking off toward the Hexrin house.

I wrap my arms around her neck as she runs, giggling with excitement. *Do not drop me, inara.*

Never, tiny witch.

ALSO FROM IVY

<u>ALIENS OF OLUURA</u>

Saving His Mate

Charming His Mate

Stealing His Mate

Keeping His Mate

Healing His Mate

Enchanting Her Mate

(This series isn't finished. There's plenty more to come!)

<u>STRANDED ON EARTH</u>

Her Alien Bodyguard

Her Alien Neighbor

Her Alien Librarian

Her Alien Student

Her Alien Boss

ENJOY THIS BOOK?

Did you enjoy this book? If so, please leave a review! It helps others find my work. Thank you for reading.

Get all the deets on new releases, bonus chapters, teasers, and giveaways by signing up for my newsletter.

FROM IVY

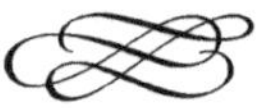

I've been teasing this pairing for a long time, and I absolutely loved the way it turned out.

Truthfully, when I first introduced each character, I had no intention of bringing them together. However, the closer Jo and Kate got, the more the idea of Jo and Alu as a couple made sense. Jo is timid and quiet, and the clan keeps their distance from the Hexrins because they don't understand their magic. So when Kate's birthday party came, and Jo was standing all alone in the corner, who would be the most likely to approach her? Alu.

Alu's lack of fear and open heart would compel her to approach a stranger who looked lonely, especially if Alu were attracted to that stranger. And because Jo and Alu are complete opposites, the spark between them would build naturally, but they'd also encounter a lot of struggles during their courtship.

Women are constantly making themselves smaller to avoid conflict, whether in their personal lives or at work, and to be honest, it's devastating to witness. Jo and Alu make themselves smaller in different ways to appease the men in their lives, and while this is a story of how they come together in love, it's also about how they find their respective voices and become more courageous.

Now, let's talk about that ending!

Jo has awakened the dead, and now a group of zombie Vikings is living among the clan. She quickly got tired of babysitting them, so she used a transference spell to make them eternally devoted to Iris instead of her. What does that mean?

It means I've got a whole new series cooking that will take place on Oluura, and Iris's story will be first! The series will be called: The Undead Vikings of Oluura and book 1 will be released in early 2023.

Don't worry, the Aliens of Oluura series isn't over. There are several more golden boys who are looking for love, and human women who have yet to be swept off their feet. The arrival of the zombie Vikings has only upped the level of competition between the two groups, and the human women have become the ultimate prize.

Stay tuned!

Love,

Ivy

P.S. - Endless hugs and smooches to my editors Tina, Mel, and Jenny, who were incredibly patient considering the tight deadline I gave them to work on this story. They were wonderful and helped me elevate Jo and Alu's love story to where it is. I owe them everything.

RESOURCES

The Trevor Project (LGBTQ+ Organization)
1-866-488-7386 (call or chat)
thetrevorproject.org/get-help/

SAMHSA (Substance Abuse and Mental Health Services
Administration Hotline)
1-800-662-HELP (4357)
TTY: 1-800-487-4889
samhsa.gov

National Suicide Prevention Hotline
1-800-273-8255 (call or chat)
suicideprevention.org

National Domestic Violence Hotline
1-800-799-SAFE (7233) (call or chat)
thehotline.org

ABOUT IVY

Ivy Knox has always been a voracious reader of romance novels, but quickly found her home in sci-fi romance because life on Earth can be kind of a drag. When she's not lost on faraway worlds created by her favorite authors, she's creating her own.

Ivy lives with her husband and two neurotic (but very cute) dogs in Chicago. When she's not reading or writing, she's probably watching *What We Do in the Shadows*, *New Girl*, *Ted Lasso*, or *Our Flag Means Death* for the millionth time.

www.ingramcontent.com/pod-product-compliance
Lightning Source LLC
Chambersburg PA
CBHW060333310726
48976CB00007B/2544